CW01460391

Bloody Festival

The young woman's nightmare begins when she is discovered with a corpse in her arms and a bloodied poker by her side. News of Luc Plouviez's murder spreads through the Brittany village of Port Briac like wildfire. But Christine Kergrist, recently jilted by Luc, swears that she had arrived just in time to comfort the dying man. Otherwise, she can offer no explanation for the terrible events of that fateful August day . . .

When Christine's fingerprints are found on the poker and the circumstantial evidence mounts against her, Jules Kergrist travels secretly to Paris. Desperate to prove his daughter's innocence, he approaches Commissaire Maximilien Orloff of the Parisian police – and Orloff agrees to take charge of an investigation where motive and evidence already provide a seemingly watertight case for the Prosecution.

Naturally suspicious of convenient explanations, Orloff begins to delve into Luc Plouviez's turbulent past. And as he interviews everyone closest to the victim, some family skeletons are deftly exposed. But another murder is committed before Orloff discovers one vital clue to a terrible family secret, a secret which finally reveals how Luc lived – and why he died . . .

Bloody Festival is an ingenious contemporary whodunnit, which provides suspense aplenty against a beautifully realised background of rural France.

BLOODY FESTIVAL

Isobel Lambot

M
MACMILLAN
LONDON

First published 1991 by
MACMILLAN LONDON LIMITED
Cavaye Place London SW10 9PG
and Basingstoke

Associated companies in Auckland, Delhi, Dublin, Gaborone,
Hamburg, Harare, Hong Kong, Johannesburg, Kuala Lumpur,
Lagos, Manzini, Melbourne, Mexico City, Nairobi, New York,
Singapore and Tokyo

ISBN 0-333-56446-4

A CIP catalogue record for this book is available from the
British Library

Typeset by Pan Macmillan Production Limited

Printed and bound in Great Britain by Billing and Sons Limited,
Worcester

Chapter 1

Luc Plouviez paid no attention to the small, tell-tale sounds behind him. His mind was filled with the joyous conviction that he was being offered a second chance. All he deserved was a kick in the pants for the sheer stupidity of rejecting a precious gift because of immature, schoolboy ideas of honour. Now, when all seemed lost, here was the gift being offered once more, and this time he would not let scruples over differences in age or his own disabled condition stand in the way.

Countless times Christine had told him these things did not matter, but in his self-disgust at not being a whole man, Luc had not listened and, as an excuse for sending her away for her own good, had seized on the need to honour a foolish promise, made as a joke to keep up spirits in a grim situation and never expected to surface in the light of day. Since then, time had dragged, the future stretching out as a dreary wilderness.

Until this day, this blessed day, August 15th, the Sainte-Marie, the Feast of the Assumption, with all France on holiday. Down the coast, at Port Briac, it was the day of the 'Pardon', the village festival. Christine always walked in the procession, wearing Breton national dress like all the other girls. He had meant to be there . . . before the dream of happiness was destroyed by his own acts.

But, incredibly, she was not in Port Briac. Luc relived the moment when he opened the shutters of a window of his living room to gaze out on the bleak rocks of Devil's Bay and saw, perched high on the eroded cliff, his lovely girl, dressed for the Festival in sombre black with delicate white lace on her head, the wind tugging and pulling at her long skirts – and his private desert burst into flowers of joy.

Luc tried to put his mind to the job in hand, simple enough, but a waste of time when there were important issues to be settled. He reminded himself to be patient, as he limped towards his desk. In the last, brief moment, he sensed a silent presence close behind but, before he had time to turn, the blow was struck to send him spinning into Eternity.

In Port Briac, the streets were quiet; the fishing boats tied up at their moorings in the rock-encircled harbour; villagers, seamen and farmers crowded into the churchyard for the Pardon, following the custom of their forebears. Religion and separatism went hand-in-hand as the priest said Mass at an open-air altar surrounded by girls in Breton dress, fishermen in navy blazers and caps and little boys in white sailor-suits, while the banners strained at their ropes in the stiffening breeze.

It was a pity about the weather. After days of hot sun, the national holiday promised little but storms on this stretch of the wild northern coast of Brittany. There was one coming, turning the sky to pewter, a sweeping cloud, dark as night, moving slowly, inexorably along the coast. Already, the fore-running winds were rustling in the trees on the other side of the graveyard, rattling round the solitary bell hanging on the top of the squat ancient church. The crowd seated in a semi-circle in front of the altar cast anxious glances seaward, as if trying to estimate how much time was left before their finery was in danger. There was general relief when the final blessing was said and the procession began to form up.

It was more like a moment of truth to a middle-aged couple, sitting hemmed in by friends and relations. The man stood up, stretching his limbs after their cramped position on hard chairs in rows set too close together. He was tall and broad, holding himself with a certain authority, as might be expected of a Brigadier of the Gendarmerie.

'Can you see Christine?' the woman enquired anxiously.

Jules Kergrist shook his head. 'They're all milling round. She'll be in there, somewhere. Don't fret, Marie,' he said, hearteningly.

His wife stood up, her fresh Breton face drained of all colour, craning her neck as if a mother's anxiety would add height to her short stature to permit her to see more than he. 'I hope you're right,' she murmured, starting to work her way through the crowd caught up in the jumble of chairs.

Gradually, the order of procession emerged from the forest of poles bearing crucifixes, flags and embroidered banners. An antique wooden carving of the Virgin was hoisted up onto a litter covered with a clean white cloth and borne aloft on the shoulders of grave-faced seamen who owed her thanks for delivery from recent peril; four little boys followed with a model of a fully-rigged ship, also on a litter; young girls brought the statue of Saint Briac, a wandering Irish monk who had fetched up in his coracle on that coast centuries ago; others fell in behind, bearing flags and flowers. The head of the procession was taken by young women in national dress, long black skirts and shawls over delicate white blouses, and hair confined under the flattish looped lace caps of that region. The notes of a solitary flute quietened the crowd, the churchyard gates were opened, and the slow progress to the harbour began.

The Kergrists watched them go, to the last straggler.

'Christine isn't there,' said Marie in flat, disappointed tones. 'I knew it. She's slipped off to see that man.'

'I thought that was all over,' Jules Kergrist muttered, more to persuade himself than in the hope that it might be the truth.

'So it should be,' his wife replied tartly. 'Luc Plouviez has made it perfectly clear that he doesn't want her. I never thought a daughter of mine would throw herself at a man.'

She sounded like the mother of a batch of girls, instead of having only one precious chick.

Kergrist sighed. He knew what was coming. 'It isn't your fault, Marie. Young people go their own way, these days.' He was in a position to know, with numbers of them falling foul of the law.

'You usually say the parents are at fault. So what've we done wrong?'

Kergrist shook his head. 'Nothing. All one can do is one's best, Marie. And stand by to pick up the pieces if things go wrong.'

'If we were given the chance! Christine won't let us get near her. She's like a stranger, haunting the house. It was better when we were quarrelling. At least, then, we were speaking to each other. I thought – ' she broke off, choking suddenly on unshed tears.

Her husband put his arm round her. 'Me too. When she dressed herself up for the procession this morning, I convinced myself that life was going back to normal.'

'This is the first time she's missed it since she was four, Jules.'

'Perhaps she's gone to see your father. She's always been fond of him.'

'She'd have said. She doesn't have to sneak off to visit him. We shouldn't have come over here today.' Marie brushed away tears. 'It was asking for trouble. It's no more than a couple of kilometres to that place. Must we do everything just because we always have?'

He could have reminded her that their annual attendance at the Pardon was rooted in her own family tradition, as witnessed by generations of ancestors buried in a line of stark stone vaults on the far side of the churchyard. By rights, Christine should be among the girls at the head of the procession, wearing her great-grandmother's lace.

'If Christine was determined to visit him today, it wouldn't have made the smallest bit of difference where we spent the holiday,' he pointed out.

'We should have gone away somewhere.'

'Now, how could we do that? It's my busiest time of the year, with the country crawling with tourists. It was difficult enough to wangle today off. And what about Christine's vacation job? She needs the extra money for next term.'

Marie Kergrist had no answer to that. With a shake of her head she walked off to join those following the procession. Her husband trailed after her. There was no comfort for either of them.

They trudged on in silence. After a while, Marie asked, 'What should we do? Wait for her?'

He shook his head. 'I expect she means to be back before the end of this. I hope she doesn't try to pretend she's been here all the time,' he added bitterly.

'I can't believe Christine would lie to us, Jules.'

'She didn't tell us she was going to slip away.'

'That's not the same as telling an outright lie.'

'Next best thing,' he growled, wondering if dressing herself up for the procession signified a genuine intention to take part or was merely deception. He glanced up at the sky. 'If she's at Devil's Bay, she'll get wet.'

'So will we,' Marie retorted, as the first flurry of stinging rain blew in across the harbour.

The procession dissolved into figures running for cover to

10

protect clothes and banners. Under the imperfect shelter of a tree, the Kergrists waited for the squall to pass, heavy drops bobbing and dancing along the road. Through it came the wail of sirens as a couple of police cars dashed past, sending up showers of spray. Then there was nothing but the menace of thunder rolling nearer.

'Let's make a dash for the car,' said Kergrist, grabbing his wife's hand. 'This could go on for an hour or more.'

She ran with him, holding her handbag up awkwardly to protect her new hair-do from the driving rain.

'Now what do we do?' she gasped, bouncing into the passenger seat. 'Christine might be soaked. We can't leave her to go home on the bus.'

'Serve her right if we did,' Kergrist snorted, but made no move to start the engine.

Presently, the fury of the storm died down and people began to emerge from shelter to re-form the procession. From across the road a young girl ran to the car, stopping short when she saw only two occupants. Recognising her as a distant cousin, the worried parents leapt out.

'Isn't Christine back?' the girl asked breathlessly. 'She borrowed my bike.'

'D'you know where she was going?' Kergrist demanded.

The girl shook her head. 'She didn't say. She meant to be back for the procession. I need my bike to go home,' she added anxiously.

'I expect she's sheltering somewhere. Don't worry. We'll find her, and the bike,' he said firmly, hustling his wife back into the car.

They drove out of Port Briac, which was little more than a village, along the coast, bumping down narrow lanes not designed for speed.

'You don't think . . . ?' Marie choked on the words she dared not utter. 'The Chasm . . .'

Kergrist read her mind, shared the dreadful fear. 'If Christine had a one-way trip in mind, she'd not have taken a bike or left that child with a long walk home.'

It was all the comfort he could offer, but Marie was not deceived. 'Those police cars . . .'

'Might have been going anywhere,' he cut her short.

They could not cover the ground fast enough. Then, at last, there it was: Devil's Bay, a strange moon-like landscape of bare rocks worn into weird shapes by the tides and storms of centuries. The place had earned its name with a long history of shipwreck – and with something more: a great fissure in the tallest rock, with sheer walls and the sea unendingly boiling at the bottom. This was The Chasm, a trap for the unwary from which there was no escape.

If Christine were a suicide, there wasn't a better spot for it in miles.

The tide was in, filling a wide shallow saucer of shingle dividing the road from the rock formations. Kergrist drove along a narrow causeway to reach the other side. There were people there – the place was a minor tourist attraction – all gathered near the police cars. These were parked some distance from The Chasm, but that was of no comfort to the Kergrists. The knot of spectators was in front of the mouth of a track, held back from entering it by a gendarme. All too well, they knew where that led – to a tall, gaunt house built on rocks overlooking the shore, the home of the man who had broken their daughter's heart, Luc Plouviez.

Kergrist hoped to God that Christine was not inside.

He got out of the car. 'Stay here, Marie. I'll scout round for her.'

'She's not with those people,' his wife pointed out in a stifled voice.

There was no one in the commonplace group who could be his lovely girl, tall like himself, slim with night-black hair halfway down her back, but, all the same, he looked carefully at the small crowd. Then he turned away to search the rock, methodically in keeping with his training, refusing to permit the now frantic parent within him to cloud his judgment.

At the foot of the climb to the top of The Chasm he found a girl's bicycle propped neatly against a large rock. He had no doubt whose property it was. Fearfully, he toiled up to the top, slipping on wet stones drying now as the sun peered out from the clouds. He forced himself to gaze down into the fissure, sharp and steep as if the great rock had been cloven by an axe.

There was no pathetic body in the bottom, mauled by the unquiet sea.

Kergrist climbed down, facing the truth which had been staring him in the face since their arrival: Christine was in that house, mixed up in whatever happening had brought a police presence to the place. And not for the first time, either. Twenty years before, tragedy had left it shuttered and empty. What had occurred now, only months after it had been re-opened?

With all his heart, Kergrist wished that Luc Plouviez had gone elsewhere to regain his health and not returned to the family property. He walked across to the track leading to the house, and its guardian, one of his own men, who came smartly to attention.

'What's going on?'

The man looked acutely uncomfortable. 'I don't know, sir.'

'Is my daughter in that house?'

'I'm not at liberty to say, Brigadier,' the man stammered. 'Shall I fetch Inspector Durieux?'

The name sent a chill down Kergrist's spine. If the *police judiciaire* were here . . . He bit back the demand to know if his girl lived or died. 'Do that, please.'

The *gendarme* abandoned his post and ran off up the track. He returned with a man in the overalls worn by a forensic team engaged in examining the scene of a crime. He ducked under the tape blocking off the entrance of the track to join Kergrist, and draw him aside, out of earshot.

They were acquainted. Alain Durieux was based in Lannion, and Kergrist knew him for a good detective, and a friend.

'For God's sake, Alain, what's happened?'

'Keep your voice down. I shouldn't even be talking to you, Jules.'

'Is Christine in there?'

'She's not hurt. We're holding her as a witness.'

'To what?'

'There's a dead man in that house. Identified as the proprietor, Luc Plouviez.'

Kergrist groaned. 'And my girl?'

'She found the body. Or so she claims. Look, Jules, go home. You can't do any good here. And don't ask me if you may see her. You know that's not possible. Shortly, she'll be taken before the *juge d'instruction*. I don't have to tell you that he makes the decisions. He'll want to see you and Marie, too. Forget you've seen me, and take my tip: get her a lawyer.'

13

Like a man in the grip of a nightmare, Kergrist returned to the car.

'What's happened?' Marie demanded, frightened by the look on his face.

He slumped into the driving seat. 'Luc's dead. They think Christine's killed him.'

Christine Kergrist gazed steadily at her legal representative. She knew his name, Marcel Landais, but this was the first time of meeting. Face to face across a bare table in a police interrogation room was hardly a social occasion.

She did not altogether like the look of him – small, and dark, with a pair of snapping black eyes which held the glint of one of Nature's predators – but she accepted that beggars could not be choosers. The Plouviez family would see to it that none of their friends or associates would defend her.

'It's good of you to take me on, Monsieur,' she said politely.

Those same eyes assessed her, but not as a woman. She was a case, a job of work, a *thing*. 'I'm encouraged that you understand your situation, Mademoiselle.'

She was still amazed that she needed a lawyer, but a long session with the police had brought home to her that her whole future was at risk. It was heart-stopping.

'I was afraid my father would have difficulty in finding someone to defend me. The Plouviez . . .' she paused, then went on, 'Tremerrec's a close-knit community.'

'You know them better than I do. I'm by way of being an outsider,' Landais said coolly.

Christine was aware that his arrival in the town, some two years earlier, had shocked the tight legal circle headed by Anatole Plouviez, Luc's cousin. They had done their best to freeze the newcomer out.

'The Plouviez family don't approve of me. I don't have the right background,' she admitted.

'Yet you persisted in your association with Luc Plouviez, despite the opposition of his family. In the end, he had to throw you out.'

Christine flinched at the brutal phrase. 'I loved him.'

'I suppose you thought you did,' Landais rapped out. 'Let's keep sentiment out of our discussion. You are in a most difficult position, Mademoiselle.'

She nodded. 'Yes, I know.'

'I wonder if you do. You were found with the dead man; your fingerprints are on the murder weapon; there are bloodstains on your clothes; and Luc Plouviez had discarded you in favour of an older woman with a lot of money. Every scrap of evidence is against you.'

'I didn't kill him,' Christine cried. 'I thought you were here to defend me?'

A thin smile touched his lips. 'I'm here to do my best for you, Mademoiselle.'

She frowned. 'So?'

'I should be doing you no service if I permitted you to beat your head against a wall. The plea of innocence will get you nowhere.'

Christine stared, aghast. 'But I *am* innocent.'

'So you say. I, in common with the police and the examining magistrate can only go on the facts. Don't entertain the notion that either the police or the *juge d'instruction* are in any way biased against you. No one wishes to see a girl of your age condemned. However, there is no other suspect in sight. I have to tell you that it is certain you will be charged with this murder.'

The day seemed to have gone on for weeks. She wondered if it would ever end, if there would be a stop to the horrors piling up on her. Every word of this dreadful little man sounded like the tolling of a funeral bell.

'I have to look at it from the point of view of the case we may present in court,' he went on inexorably. 'We have only your word against a great deal of unassailable forensic evidence, none of which you are in a position to deny.'

She took a deep breath to conquer the blind panic which threatened to engulf her. 'I haven't tried to deny anything except the accusation of murder. When I went to Port Briac this morning, I had no thought of doing anything other than attending the Pardon. I'd no intention of going to Devil's Bay. It was a spur-of-the-moment decision. I found Luc on the floor and I thought he was dead. He wasn't, quite. He died in my arms.'

Landais sighed. 'It's a pity he didn't tell you who'd done it.'

'He was too far gone.'

'Why did you touch the murder weapon?'

Christine shook her head. 'I don't know. It was lying on the carpet. I didn't think.'

'Manifestly not,' retorted Landais, drily. 'If your fingerprints weren't on that poker, we might have a ghost of a chance with the plea of innocence. As it is, we haven't a prayer.'

'But surely, if I had killed Luc –' she all but choked over the word – 'I would've wiped the weapon?'

'The Prosecution will counter that by pointing out that you were not expecting anyone to walk in on you, that if Madame Foucard, the woman who ousted you in the affections of Luc Plouviez, had not come to the house, you would have cleaned up all traces of your own presence.'

The scene flashed in front of Christine's eyes – her own grief, holding tightly on to the body of her dead love as if their farewell must last forever – and then a scream and the sight of a total stranger standing in the doorway . . .

'My advice to you, Mademoiselle, is to plead guilty in a moment of passion, and let me persuade the court to take into account your youth, your inexperience, the harsh treatment you received at the hands of Luc Plouviez; to ask, in effect, for mercy. Frenchmen are never insensible to the appeal of beauty in distress.'

The nearest in blood to the murdered man, Anatole Plouviez and his sister, Simone Tremel, together with their respective spouses and offspring, invariably spent the Sainte-Marie in a family gathering. The Tremels lived an elevated existence in Rennes, making a point of visiting Brittany every August, arriving in time for the Feast and staying on until the end of the month.

Rarely was it a happy reunion, although they had much in common. Anatole and Simone's husband were both well-established and competent lawyers, but Louis Tremel regarded his brother-in-law as one of a lesser breed, a fact that would have enraged a far less self-important individual. Armed truce reigned for this one occasion when they were together, since there were two extremely aged and well-heeled aunts to be buttered up by both sides. They had a common fear that the property might be left to charity, and the Tremels a particular one that Anatole might succeed in getting an edge over them if they neglected the family tradition. By way of countering this, they insisted on staying the whole fortnight with the aunts at their estate downstream from Tremerrec.

The entertainment on the feast-day consisted of Mass at the Cathedral, then a trip on Anatole's boat and a picnic on one of the islands at the mouth of the river. Frequently this turned out a disaster, but the aunts enjoyed it – the Plouviez family had always put out to sea on this national holiday – and being deaf knew nothing of the barbed comments and undercurrents of animosity circulating among the younger generations.

This year, the Tremel teenagers had insisted on a barbecue instead of the old-fashioned picnic, a recipe for certain disaster in Anatole's opinion. For once, he did not voice it, perceiving an opportunity of discrediting his rivals for the inheritance but, in the event, the quarrel which erupted in his own house on the morning of the festivities made sure that the old ladies' day out was ruined from the start, and went from bad to worse.

Weary and out of temper with the whole world, Anatole returned home to find a police car waiting outside. It was all he needed . . .

Simone came alone in response to his telephone call, the ineffable Louis preferring to shun any contact with sordid crime. She stomped into the house.

No one could ever mistake the relationship between the two. Likeness was stamped on their strong, sturdy frames, bulldog faces and loud, overbearing voices. They had their differences, past and present, but Anatole knew his sister could be relied upon in a crisis. Briefly, he recited the facts.

Simone, being the elder by two years, made the decisions. 'Louis and the children will go home in the morning. I'll stay on for a day or two, though the case sounds straightforward enough. You say the girl was caught red-handed?'

'So I'm told. What should we do about Luc's fiancée?'

Simone shrugged. 'The least possible.'

'But she will be shattered,' Anatole protested.

'Not she. That woman's an adventuress. Did Luc make a will in her favour?'

'No, the old one is still valid. The property goes to charity,' he added dismally.

'Better that than into Marguerite Foucard's hands,' she replied briskly. 'Don't make a fuss, Anatole. The first job is to inform the family. Make a list and we'll each do half. Forget La Foucard. I'd be very surprised to find *her* doing much grieving.'

Regretfully Anatole toed the line. He had fancied a trip back into town to comfort the bereaved lady . . .

Marcel Landais drove back to Tremerrec in a jaunty mood. He was an up-and-coming man, not one to miss an opportunity such as this. A bravura performance in court would show the stuffed shirts of the town's legal establishment – a closed shop if ever there was one – that he was a force to be reckoned with, a smart operator to whom clients would flock, once his reputation was made.

It would be a big advance on defending shoplifters, wayward motorists and the occasional petty thief, on whom he had been obliged to waste his talents in the couple of years since his migration from Paris.

Brittany, the land of his mother's people, was his chosen field for the advancement of his career. Since he did nothing by halves, he had gone slightly over the top on the separatism bit, receiving a nasty setback when he discovered that the Bretons did not take readily to strangers claiming to be one of themselves. But Landais was not easily discouraged. He was looking for the right sort of bride, the daughter of an impeccably Breton family, with a good dowry. Tremerrec could offer several candidates, but none were available to him until he could penetrate the top level of the town's society.

Christine Kergrist seemed to bring everything within his grasp. Her father, the officer in charge of the *gendarmerie* at Tremerrec, was universally respected. Had the murder victim been anyone else, Anatole Plouviez, the doyen of the legal profession, would have undertaken the defence. As it was, allowing for the fact that none of the other lawyers would touch her case with a bargepole, he, Marcel Landais, was the only local man to whom the Brigadier could turn.

It was all highly satisfactory – as long as the girl did not persist in her idiotic claim of innocence. He hoped he had made her understand the exact position.

He dismissed from his mind the notion that she might stand firm. The assertion would be made in panic at being discovered with her victim, and stuck to out of female perversity. Satisfied that he had the truth of the matter, and therefore could deal with it, he drove straight to the Kergrist house, arriving there in the early evening of that fateful day.

18

Tremerrec was a small, ancient town at the head of navigation of a broad river estuary. From the wharfs, the narrow streets rose steeply to the town square and the airy Gothic Cathedral with its soaring lacy spire. The Kergrists lived in the heart of the old town, in a tall stone and timber building, the family home for the past two hundred years, where shoe-making had earned their bread until the twentieth century swept the old ways into the history books. The interior was on the dark side, made more so by heavy oak furniture of considerable age which took the lawyer's covetous eye. It embodied the Breton solidity he hoped to create for his own descendants.

Kergrist led him into a stuffy parlour which had the air of being used chiefly for gatherings of mourners. Landais discovered that the solid ancient chairs with horsehair seats were distinctly lacking in comfort. He reminded himself not to wriggle, as Madame Kergrist joined them, slipping quietly into the room. She sat in one corner, hands tightly clasped in her lap, her eyes fixed on him in painful hope.

The Brigadier wore much the same expression, but without the optimism. 'How bad is it?' he asked heavily.

Landais glanced from one to the other and settled on the husband. 'I've seen Mademoiselle Christine, Monsieur, and spoken with officers of the *police judiciaire* – '

'Is Alain Durieux in charge of the case still?' Kergrist broke in.

'He is. Your own good reputation as a police officer is standing us in good stead. I have received much cooperation.'

Marie Kergrist drew in her breath sharply. Landais glanced at her with some compassion. 'There's no way I can make this easy for you, Madame. Let me give you the facts. Around half past eleven this morning, your daughter was found kneeling beside the body of a dead man. He had been battered to death with a poker.'

'What has Christine to say to that?' Kergrist demanded.

'She pleads innocence, Monsieur. She says she found him barely alive and he died in her arms a moment later. Her fingerprints are on the murder weapon. She admits to being in love with the victim, who appears to have thrown her over and announced his engagement to a woman nearer his own age. The deceased was forty – '

'Christine won't be twenty until December,' Marie wailed.

'Why didn't she send for help?' Kergrist asked, frowning.

'She insists she was about to do that, when the fiancée, Marguerite Foucard, who arrived from Paris this morning, walked in on her.' Landais paused, then added, 'The *juge d'instruction* is satisfied that the girl has a case to answer. I'm sorry, Monsieur. The *crime passionnel* has a fascination, you understand.'

Kergrist glanced briefly at his wife, who sat with her handkerchief pressed to her mouth to cover her distress. 'Will you act for her, Monsieur?'

The lawyer inclined his head in what was almost a small bow. 'Certainly. I will do my best for her, Brigadier. She will make a good impression in court: young, pretty, vulnerable. A man would have to have a very strong deterrent to discard such a creature. The fiancée is a divorcée, mature, elegant, and, I suspect, rich.'

Kergrist had had as much as he could stomach. He asked only one more question, then set himself to getting rid of the man without antagonising him.

'When can we see Christine?'

Landais raised a hand in a silent appeal for patience. 'Tomorrow, I hope. If the *juge* permits.'

The moment he had gone, Marie burst out, 'He thinks she did it.'

'He's not alone. Not one of them is looking further than the end of his nose. But don't worry, love. I'm not about to let anyone railroad Christine into prison. I'll think of something.'

Chapter 2

The murder of Luc Plouviez caused a great stir in Tremerrec and district, rousing old memories of the eccentric man who, some thirty years before, had built the house at Devil's Bay in the teeth of opposition from a number of persons and organisations. Uncle Emile Plouviez had made many enemies in the course of desecrating a place of natural wild and fearful beauty with an outstandingly ugly building. Death had struck the offender down, eventually, and now a second tragedy set in motion whispers of perpetual bad luck.

The Kergrists retreated behind their own defences. Marie was rarely seen, and took to driving to Paimpol to do the shopping. The Brigadier did his duty doggedly, and few dared approach him. No one was surprised when he applied for a short leave of absence.

Anatole Plouviez deserted his office, spending days in a virtual state of siege in his luxurious home overlooking the river, upstream from the town. The telephone hardly stopped ringing, as relations – and there were a good many of them – clamoured for news. He was supported by his sister, his own wife, Yvonne, being too overcome by events to be of help to anyone. Anatole and Simone left her to droop in the kitchen, well aware that her distress was not primarily for the departed Luc. She was a thin, washed-out woman, who had been crushed by this formidable pair for twenty-five years. No sort of action from her was expected.

She therefore surprised them, offering resistance to their joint solution to an urgent problem. 'No, Anatole, I know Simone is making the offer out of the best of intentions, but I really can't agree that Sacha should go back with her to Rennes.'

Brother and sister stared. It was as if a piece of furniture had suddenly spoken up. Between them, they had been settling the immediate future of the son of the house, a precious only child who was a grievous disappointment to his father, and never more so than in this moment of family distress.

Yvonne seized her momentary advantage and pressed on: 'Sacha's very upset about Christine. It's no good pretending he isn't still in love with her, in spite of everything. He needs support, not being shovelled out of the way. He's our son and we're the ones who should give it.'

Her husband and sister-in-law understood the 'we' to be conventional. Yvonne was referring only to herself. Taken aback by her own audacity, she paused – and lost her edge.

Recovering himself, Anatole jumped in, 'This is what comes of molly-coddling him, keeping him at home instead of sending him away to a decent school.'

His wife rose up in defence of the national system of education – hadn't her own father been a teacher? – 'Sacha wouldn't have done any better elsewhere.'

'He wouldn't have spent years in the same classroom as Christine Kergrist,' he snapped back, grimly.

'I don't give a sou for an education which doesn't teach students to think.' Simone Tremel could not bear to be left out of an argument. 'The evidence makes the girl's guilt perfectly clear.'

'I don't like to see my son making a fool of himself,' Anatole added. 'It really won't do to have him constantly pestering the police.'

Yvonne had no answer to that. Sacha was passing hours a day on the steps of the *police judiciaire* offices.

'He'll be better away from here for a time,' Simone pointed out. 'It'll be useful experience for him to work for us, too.'

'You and Louis might even make a lawyer of him,' said Anatole in a heavy-handed attempt at a joke.

Yvonne shot him a weary glance. 'All Sacha has ever wanted to do is go to sea,' she said, in a last flicker of spirit. 'And to marry Christine Kergrist.'

This was too much for her husband. 'Over my dead body,' he roared. 'Sacha goes to Rennes tomorrow.'

A week after her daughter was charged with the murder of Luc Plouviez, Marie Kergrist drove alone to the prison for the visiting hour. It felt uncomfortable without Jules, and she was worried but she did her best to hide it from Christine.

'Are they treating you well?' she asked fatuously, scanning the girl's pale face which seemed to have grown thinner since her last visit.

Christine brushed the question aside. 'What's happening? I hear no news.'

'Sacha Plouviez gave me a message for you. Oh, no, please listen,' Marie said urgently, as her daughter's hand moved in an involuntary gesture of rejection. 'He's on your side. He's been making a nuisance of himself to Alain, insisting on your innocence and demanding to see you.'

'That must please his father.'

'He packed Sacha off to Rennes yesterday to stay with the Tremels.'

The ice melted a little. 'Poor Sacha! Between his father insisting on him studying law and all this impossible devotion to me, he doesn't have much luck, does he? Where's Papa?'

The sudden switch took her mother by surprise. She forgot the prepared excuse and faltered.

Christine's eyes glittered. 'Where is he, Maman? You must tell me.'

Marie hesitated, then said, 'He's in Paris.'

'What's he doing there?' Steady eyes examined fresh lines on her mother's face. 'Don't palm me off with any rot about visiting friends.'

Marie was ashamed to feel so relieved. Bottling it up had done her no good at all. 'He's gone to see Commissaire Orloff.'

Christine sat very still. 'Why?'

'To ask for help. For you.'

'From that man? Orloff put Papa through hoops when he was in Tremerrec. He gave the whole brigade a hard time.'

'Who told you that?' Marie demanded, diverted for a moment.

'There was an endless stream of wives coming to complain to you over the long hours their husbands had to work, and how demanding the Commissaire was. I heard most of it.'

'You always did have long ears. It's perfectly true that Monsieur Orloff makes his own rules, but he gets results,' Marie said, bravely talking down her fears by quoting her husband's own words. 'Your father admires him greatly.'

Christine gazed at her in consternation. 'Is it all right for Papa to go to Paris to ask the Commissaire for help?'

Miserably, Marie shook her head. 'No, it isn't. If anyone found out, it could cost him his job. Christine, I'm so worried. This trip is madness, but he would go and I can't see that it'll do any good, either.'

The girl's shoulders drooped. 'He shouldn't have done it. I'm just not worth that much risk.'

Marie choked back a sob. 'We love you. You're all we have.'

It seemed to her that Christine drew back. 'I'm bringing you nothing but grief.'

'Every family goes through difficult times. It's easier if they stick together.'

The girl shook her head. 'Not for me, if it's at the cost of Papa's job and your security with it. I have to do this alone. Please try to understand.'

Marie's heart came up into her mouth. What did that mean?

The address was a suburban street. Never had Kergrist felt less sure of himself, nor more of an alien presence, the typical country hick come up to Paris. He stared at a three-storey house, built perhaps a hundred years ago, one of a terrace, but distinguished from the rest by the possession of a carriage entrance. The double doors were firmly shut, one of them pierced by a panel to admit pedestrians, and bearing a bellpush.

Scrutiny of neighbouring houses had told him that most were divided into apartments. But not this one. There was one bell, and one name above it: Orloff.

Kergrist hesitated, although there remained barely a minute before the hour of his appointment. This was the point of no return. Once inside, stating his business, he would be putting at risk his entire career. No one back home in Brittany would accept that a mere Brigadier was entitled to go over the heads of all and sundry to enlist the help of a highly-placed officer of the *police judiciaire*.

If, indeed, Orloff would listen to him.

He plucked up his courage and pressed the bell, buoyed up by the recollection that the Commissaire had caught on at lightning speed when Kergrist telephoned. And wasn't the fact that Orloff had invited him to come to his private address rather than his office a proof of utmost tact and appreciation of the delicate nature of the Brigadier's request?

A small door opened, and a voice he remembered well invited him to step in. The archway was dim, the end blocked by garage doors. In the gloom, Kergrist made out the imposing figure of the Commissaire.

'It's very good of you to see me,' he began, as Orloff conducted him to the front door in the left-hand wall.

Kergrist found himself in a narrow hall, where daylight penetrated solely through doors opening off it, discreetly lit by wall lights which struck fire from a splendid icon of the Virgin and Child, ornamented with gold and precious stones. Once he could wrench his eyes away from it, he perceived below it a small console table bearing a framed and signed photograph of the doomed last Tsar of All the Russias. The effect was daunting and Kergrist pinched his leg to remind himself that this was Paris and not Moscow.

His host flung open a door, and the clear light of a summer evening swept away the claustrophobic dimness; the icon returned to being a work of art; and the dead Nicholas was revealed as a mild and pleasant-looking man in fading sepia.

Orloff ushered his guest into a room at the back of the house, where long windows opened on to a small, lush garden. The heavy scent of old-fashioned roses filled the air. Kergrist sat down carefully on a chair his year's salary might buy, at a pinch. To his untrained eye, every piece looked as if it belonged in a museum, the whole scenario hardly typical of the home life of the average cop.

But Maximilien Orloff was never that . . .

He was busy pouring drinks, a huge man but not gross, with springy light brown hair, wearing casual lightweight clothes which were a long way from Kergrist's own off-the-peg slacks and shirt. He handed his guest a glass, gazing at him speculatively out of bright blue eyes under jutting brows.

The informality of it, the unfamiliar setting, a sense of being out of time and place, made Kergrist nervous. He recalled that the Commissaire on duty was an unsettling presence; here, in his own home, doubly so. The Brigadier, feeling himself to be a simple Breton peasant in the face of lost grandeur, longed for the familiar discomfort of official buildings.

'It's very good of you to see me,' he repeated, and added, 'It's all rather irregular.'

Orloff smiled. 'I thought it better to drag you all the way out here. Your presence at my office would have been noted.'

'I appreciate that, Commissaire.' Kergrist drew a deep breath. 'I've no business to be here at all.'

'A great stepping on the toes of your superior officers,' Orloff agreed cheerfully. 'What can I do for you?'

'It's my daughter, Christine. She's in trouble.' He stopped, hardly knowing where to begin.

Orloff eased his path. 'Let me tell you that I know a little of the matter, Brigadier. From what I remembered of you, I assumed there had to be some serious difficulty which prompted your approach to me. So I have put myself in possession of the salient facts. However, I would prefer that you told me the whole story in your own way.' He smiled again, a beguiling smile which Kergrist knew was used unscrupulously to persuade people to Orloff's will. 'In every little detail, please. You will remember my addiction to details.'

Kergrist felt heartened. This was why he had come: for Orloff to pinpoint the detail which would save Christine.

'My daughter's nearly twenty, a bright girl. She's at university, studying medicine, doing well, too. At least, she was until a few months ago. She came home for the Easter vacation, and had the bad luck to meet Luc Plouviez.'

'How did that come about?'

'Through his cousin's son, a lad she's known all her life. From the Lycée, of course. We're not on visiting terms with the Plouviez family,' said Kergrist with a wry smile.

He would have plunged on, but Orloff stopped him. 'Tell me about them. Do they live in Tremerrec?'

'All except Luc. The family came from Port Briac. That's a place not far from Devil's Bay.' Kergrist sighed. 'We were there that morning, at the Pardon. My wife's home's near there. We always go to the Pardon. Christine came with us, but slipped off without telling us, borrowed a kid's bike and pedalled over to see Luc. She never came back.'

'If your daughter was intent on visiting the man that day, she would have done it no matter where you were,' Orloff pointed out, going straight to the unspoken guilt. 'Don't blame yourselves for being in the vicinity.'

'My wife does. She's so proud of Christine. So am I. It's a

great thing for people like us to have a child studying to be a doctor.' He broke off, ashamed at showing emotion. 'This is wasting your time.'

Orloff shook his head slightly. 'You were telling me about the Plouviez family.'

'They were fishermen, originally,' said Kergrist, with an attempt at a dispassionate official voice. 'Sometime last century one of the sons broke free, took himself off to the colonies and made a pile. Eventually, he came back to Port Briac, built himself a house, married and settled down to live on his *rentes*. You may imagine what happened. Within a couple of generations, the Plouviez had forgotten about being fishermen, moved into Tremerrec and worked their way into the best circles. The family practise law now.'

'Which one of them went to live at Devil's Bay? A strange choice, I'm told.'

'That was Emile Plouviez, thirty-odd years ago. He was the youngest of three brothers, couldn't stand the stuffy respectability of the family and ran away to sea. He made a fortune in the Far East – no one knows how, best not ask – came back to Brittany in his fifties, promptly quarrelled with his relations as well as a good many others, and put up that monstrosity.'

'An ugly house?'

'A tall, gaunt place, right on the rocks, as near as he could get to The Chasm – that's what the house is called too, though it's beyond me why anyone should want to live there. There are endless complaints about it spoiling the view.'

'How did Luc acquire it?'

'The old man left it to him. Luc gained his favour by joining the Navy. The place has been shut up for years, with Luc away at sea. He came home last winter, invalided out of the service, with his leg shot to pieces after some accident aboard ship.' Bitterness and pain suddenly welled up, cracking the man's hard-won calm. 'What the blazes can have got into Christine to go mooning after a cripple old enough to be her father? She's not just clever, Commissaire, she's beautiful. She didn't have to throw herself away on him.'

'No doubt her medical interest was aroused, initially. And girls are often fascinated by older men,' said Orloff.

Kergrist had a swift vision of young women by the score trailing after the Commissaire. There was no sign of the female touch in this house, but it wouldn't be for lack of trying. In his social circle – and what might that be? – Orloff must rank as a prime catch.

'He'd turned forty,' Kergrist went on. 'I never met him. I suppose he was charming, man-of-the-world and all that. Christine was besotted with him.'

'Why didn't you meet him? Most parents seem obliged to put up with whatever their children bring home, no matter how undesirable.'

'Luc Plouviez hardly came into that category,' Kergrist replied bitterly. 'He wasn't a dropout. We asked Christine to invite him. She refused.'

'D'you know why?'

There was a short pause, then the Brigadier sighed: 'What's the modern phrase? Breakdown of communications? Since she came home for the long vacation, we haven't been able to talk the way we used to.'

'So, in fact, you can only speak for your daughter's feelings. You don't know, at first hand, the man's attitude. Only what she told you.'

Kergrist brightened a little. 'No, that's true, Commissaire. But why would she insist that he loved her if he hadn't said so?'

'Wishful thinking, reading more into the situation than was actually there. Unfortunately, that doesn't constitute a defence against the charges she's facing.'

Once more, gloom engulfed the stricken father. 'It doesn't matter what he said, it's what he did that counts. Christine's mistake was to believe him. My own opinion is, he tolerated her infatuation, took advantage of it. She was useful about the place and always on hand to change the dressings on his leg. The crunch came when, out of the blue, he suddenly announced his engagement to that Foucard woman. Christine was shattered. She still didn't believe it, the day of the Pardon. She swears that's why she went to see him. To convince herself.' He stood up. 'I shouldn't have come, Commissaire. But thank you for listening to me. It's helped to talk, and there's nothing I want to say to Inspector Durieux. To be fair, he doesn't expect me to volunteer evidence against my own daughter.'

'It would appear that Durieux is doing no less than his duty in arresting Mademoiselle Christine. In the light of the existing evidence.'

28

The words held an awful note of finality, of an appeal rejected by the highest court.

Surprisingly, Orloff continued, 'On the other hand, there is one small matter of special interest in this case, which shall have my attention. But, I must warn you, Brigadier, I can promise nothing.'

Kergrist was baffled. It seemed too easy. 'What matter of special interest?' he ventured.

The famous smile reappeared. 'Just one little point I must check on. Tell me, had Luc Plouviez retired from the Navy?'

'He'd hardly be fit for active service. He'd lost one leg and the other was in a bad state. I suppose he could've been in line for a desk job,' the Brigadier replied doubtfully.

'He was a senior officer. A Captain.'

'Was he? Christine never said. I don't know why that should surprise me but it does. He must've been damned good to make that rank by the age of forty.'

'Interesting, isn't it?' said Orloff. 'What do you know about his fiancée, Marguerite Foucard?'

Kergrist shook his head. 'Damn all. She appeared out of the blue. I've seen her once or twice, a very striking-looking woman.'

'Indeed, she is, Brigadier. Is she still in Tremerrec?'

Curiosity seized Kergrist, amazed that the Commissaire should know of the woman. Was she the 'special interest'? And in what way: professional or personal? He wished he dared ask.

'She comes and goes, I'm told,' he said cautiously. 'We keep a check on the hotels.'

'You might do us both a favour if you could find out if she has associations – other than the late Luc Plouviez – with Brittany.'

So it was professional interest, or maybe a bit of both. Madame Foucard carried herself with the air of a woman of consequence. Jules Kergrist went home filled with satisfaction at having succeeded in catching Orloff's interest, but as the train covered the long miles, other ideas began to float up to the surface of his mind. Perhaps it had been too easy . . . the Commissaire was not a man to be persuaded by a father's grief unless there was something in it for him . . . and what was behind his strange questions over Luc Plouviez and Marguerite Foucard? Both had presented an appearance of respectability and wealth.

29

By the time he left the train at Guingamp, Kergrist had persuaded himself that, far from helping Christine, he would be used in one of the Commissaire's own devious games, and once he had handed over the information, that would be the end of Orloff's involvement and Christine would be left to her fate.

Anatole Plouviez was feasting his eyes on the woman seated in the client's chair on the other side of his desk. He liked ladies to have a bit of flesh on their bones and, being on the short side himself, had a taste for the statuesque. Marguerite Foucard amply filled both requirements, with the additional attractions of a luscious olive skin and thick shiny black hair, cleverly sculpted by her *coiffeur*, but which Anatole could imagine hanging halfway down her back.

The thought sent shivers – of what? anticipation? delicious panic? – down his back. He could have wished that her dark eyes held a languorous gleam rather than the sharpness which restrained him from leaping round the desk to fondle her plump ring-laden hand. With an inward sigh, he recognised that this was a businesswoman of no mean acumen.

'Luc's house,' she said crisply. 'I want to buy it.'

Visions of what might be in store for him with this gorgeous creature resident in the vicinity threatened to clog his mental processes. But only for the briefest of moments, as other aspects of this proposed purchase began to sink in.

'I suppose it will be put up for sale,' Marguerite went on.

'I'm not in a position to tell you, Madame. As you know, Luc left it to a charity. I imagine they will want to sell. I can't see that the house would be of any particular use to them. It's not big enough for a residential home, apart from being in an inconvenient place. Even the water has to come from the farm up the lane.'

He wondered why she should want the place. The lonely house at Devil's Bay was an unlikely setting for this bird of paradise.

Marguerite Foucard seemed to read his mind. 'I've a sentimental attachment, you understand, Monsieur. It was where my poor Luc died.'

That was a jolt. In the course of his career Anatole had dealt with many bereaved ladies. Some, indeed, had wished to make a shrine of the dear departed's house, often to the intense irritation of other members of the family who would share the gains from a

30

sale of the property. He had thought he could pick out the true sentimentalist at a hundred paces' distance, and would not have numbered his visitor among them – not at her undisclosed but mature age and with at least one marriage behind her.

'Your sensibility does you credit, Madame, but that house is so isolated,' he began, and pulled himself up short. It was not in his interest to discourage her: a lonely lady would need a comforter.

'I'm not afraid of being alone,' Marguerite replied, shortly. She rose. 'Perhaps you'd be so good as to inform my lawyer if and when the house comes onto the market,' she added, laying a card on the desk and was out of the door with the briefest of farewells and down the corridor with a remarkable turn of speed which foiled her admirer's pursuit.

Anatole swallowed his disappointment at not having time to lay so much as a finger on that inviting flesh. He consoled himself with the reflection that Marguerite Foucard's entry into the market for Luc's house would annoy his sister.

For a moment he brooded over the forceful Simone Tremel. For as long as he could remember she had bossed him about, generally, he was obliged to admit, to his advantage. He had been glad enough for her to get Sacha out of the way, but Anatole was not at all sure that he fancied the idea of her owning a house so close to Tremerrec. What was bought as a holiday home could turn into a permanent residence. He picked up the telephone.

'You've competition over Luc's house,' he announced.

'You mean, you can't persuade the charity to go for a private sale,' Simone replied tartly. 'Didn't you explain to them that it could be a difficult place to sell?'

'There's another interested party. Marguerite.'

'Is she still around? I thought she'd gone home after the funeral. What does she want with the house?'

'It's the place where Luc died. She wants to feel near to him.'

'Stuff and nonsense,' Simone snorted. 'That woman hasn't a sentimental bone in her body.'

'She can run up the price.'

'She won't outbid me. It'll be a commercial proposition to her. I shouldn't be surprised if it isn't your fault. Luc is sure to have told her about the time you wanted him to sell the house to you to turn into holiday flats.'

31

'I can't understand why *you* want it,' Anatole replied, nettled.

'It's family property. Luc had no business to leave it to outsiders.'

'It was his to do as he pleased,' her brother pointed out.

'Luc never did have a sense of what is due to the family,' Simone retorted. 'It will do very well as a holiday home for us. We can't go on staying with the aunts every year.'

'You have done so ever since you married Louis. Twenty years,' Anatole reminded her.

'The aunts are very old. Once they go, I'm sure Yvonne wouldn't be at all pleased to have us descending on her.'

'It'd put high-and-mighty Louis's nose out of joint.'

'He's a very private person,' Simone corrected her brother, coldly. 'With the highest of standards.'

'You could buy the estate when the old women push off.'

'How very coarse you are, Anatole. I've no intention of doing any such thing. Places on the river are much too expensive.'

'Even when they're in the family?'

'You can't compare the two properties. Luc's house was built by Uncle Emile. The aunts' place was bought to house them after their husbands had died. You can't class that as family property.'

There was never any arguing with Simone. 'You'll have to fight it out with Madame Foucard,' he said grumpily.

'I'm relying on you to discourage her. Don't be taken in when that woman flaps her false eyelashes at you. I'm not blind, Anatole, I've seen you slobbering over her. She'll only make a fool of you.'

Anatole was so affronted by this attack on his latest object of desire that he threw in, as extra ammunition, an item of gossip which he had heard that morning. 'Marguerite will have to stay on here. I'm told there's a *police judiciaire* Commissaire coming from Paris to review the investigation into Luc's death.'

The bolt misfired. 'Then I'd better come, too,' Simone said grimly. 'There's been enough scandal over Luc's murder without you adding to it.'

Chapter 3

Alain Durieux stood stiffly, almost to attention, confronting his unwelcome visitor. Commissaire Orloff's last excursion into Brittany had happened before his own appointment to the *police judiciaire* in Lannion, but he had heard all about it, and the tale had lost nothing in the telling.

'All precautions were taken to prevent contamination of the scene of the crime,' he said in an arctic voice. 'I stand by everything my team did. The procedures were entirely correct. Whoever has laid a complaint against me or any of my men has acted out of ignorance or malice.'

They were standing in the bare room allotted to the Commissaire for use during his investigation. There was a desk, a few chairs and a filing cabinet. The Inspector had waited only long enough to close the door against long ears outside before launching into speech. Orloff understood exactly what the matter was: good cops invariably resented his intrusion into their lives.

Durieux was dwarfed by him but that, too, was usual. The Commissaire stood well over six feet, and broad with it. The Inspector was a middle-sized, compact man, with brown hair and a toothbrush moustache, and a flattish face with a wide jaw. Orloff guessed there were fires behind the correct exterior. He had no desire to poke them into a flare-up.

He walked round the desk and laid his briefcase beside a waiting pile of folders.

'There's no disciplinary element in this, Inspector,' he said mildly. 'No one has lodged a complaint. Who did you think might have done?'

Durieux hesitated. 'I'd rather not say.'

Orloff sat down. 'Since you raised the matter, I rather think you should.'

'I've no evidence, only a suspicion.'

'You may tell me, then I'll make sure I don't fall foul of them, myself,' the Commissaire replied, with a faint hint of mockery which earned him a doubtful glance. 'Who is it?'

'Maître Landais, the girl's lawyer. He's a sharp customer.'

'Ah, I see. You think a complaint lodged against the police handling of the case might be a smart defence ploy to create doubt well in advance of any trial?'

'It has crossed my mind,' Durieux admitted.

'Then maybe you're one stage sharper than Monsieur Landais, Inspector. If he's trying to pull any such stunt, it hasn't come to my ears. Rest assured, the Minister doesn't send me out to investigate complaints – only on matters of possibly special interest.'

Durieux shot him a look of deepest suspicion. 'I can't see anything special about this crime, Commissaire. Everything points to the girl's guilt.'

Orloff smiled faintly. 'I understand the question you don't feel you can ask, Inspector. I'm quite accustomed to being regarded as an unwelcome intruder. Please bear with me.'

Acutely embarrassed, Durieux flushed. 'My apologies, Commissaire. I promise you all the help you need from me.'

The smile broadened. It had a quality which made the Inspector blink. 'I never doubted that for a moment,' said Orloff gently.

'But there isn't another suspect in sight,' Durieux surprised himself by blurting out what was, for him, the heart of the problem. 'If there were, I'd have gone straight after them. I've known Christine Kergrist since she was a kid. I was at school with her father. Our families are close – or *were*,' he added, with a painful plunge into human emotion over the certain loss of an old friend. 'My wife's her godmother.'

There was a knock on the door. Displeased, Durieux shouted to the flouter of his orders to go away, and that they were not to be disturbed. There was a tiny pause, then another, more insistent knock. With a smothered oath, the Inspector slipped outside.

He was back in an instant. 'Madame Foucard, the victim's fiancée, is here, making a nuisance of herself. She's trying to gain admission to the murder house, to pick up things she claims are hers. She's a persistent old bag. What can I tell her?'

The Commissaire was amused at some private joke. 'She's one of the people I want to see. Have her brought in, please.'

Marguerite stalked in like a diva making an entrance on stage to a theatreful of fans. She was superb in every way, top-to-toe a work of art, of uncertain age under the paint, lovely curves caressed by the sort of 'little' dress obtainable only from a top couturier.

Her imperious gaze swept the room, landing on Orloff. She halted abruptly, and behind her, Durieux was obliged to step aside quickly to avoid cannoning into her.

'You!' she exclaimed.

The Commissaire was on his feet. 'What a pleasure to meet you again, Madame. Please sit down.'

She arranged herself on a hard government-issue chair, taking time to recover from the nasty shock. 'I didn't expect the great Orloff to bother about a sordid crime of passion,' she said acidly.

'How could I resist, when your name was mentioned?' he replied, with a hint of mockery.

Durieux, occupying an inconspicuous seat against a wall, sat up, suddenly interested.

The Commissaire resumed his seat. 'I was surprised to hear you were intending to remarry, Madame. And to an obscure ex-naval officer. One wonders how the two of you met.'

Marguerite shrugged. Anatole Plouviez would have appreciated the sinuous movement of those shoulders, which was wasted upon Orloff. 'People meet in all sorts of places. It's none of your business, Commissaire.' She twisted round to give Durieux a hard stare. 'How long do I have to wait to retrieve my own property?'

Orloff intervened. 'I regret, Madame, but we have not yet finished with the house.'

'You're looking for some means of persecuting me,' she flashed back at him. 'Luc Plouviez and I weren't engaged in any business deals. If you must know, I'd decided it was time to settle down.'

'Not surely due to advancing age, Madame? I thought you were forever young.'

Marguerite pressed her lips together at the open jibe. She decided to ignore it. 'I had no part in Luc's death, Commissaire, unless you count putting that girl's nose out of joint. Inspector Durieux investigated my movements thoroughly. I was on my way here when he was killed. And I can prove it.' She paused, then added resentfully, 'I suppose it's too much to hope you'll let me go home with or without my things?'

'I'm glad I don't have to spell it out to you, Madame. Please remain at your hotel for the time being. You are free to go now. I shall want to see you again very soon.'

Marguerite stood up. 'Bastard!' she flung at him and marched out.

Durieux was on his feet. 'Shall I put a tail on her? She might skip.'

Orloff shook his head. 'She's much too bright for that. She'll stay put. She knows she has to, if she wants to get rid of me.'

'Who is she? I didn't think of investigating her background. She seemed right out of it.'

'She's the divorced wife of Georges Foucard, a rich industrialist and financier, with a finger in pies all over the world.'

'How did she let him escape from her grip? That one's an expensive type.'

'I'm told it was all very amicable. I imagine the poor fellow found her a bit too much for him. He set her up with a lot of property as a settlement. He'll also back her if she finds herself in trouble – as she has on a couple of occasions – and he can pull strings at the highest level. She's Lebanese, and trading seems to be in her blood. She doesn't need the money, but she amuses herself by dabbling.'

The Inspector relaxed so far as to grin at the Commissaire's tone. 'In what?'

'Now you're asking. At one time, she was suspected of dealing in illicit diamonds but nothing was proved. She spends a lot of her time in the Middle East.'

'She might be into drugs.'

'Indeed, so. Or gun-running. Or both. La Foucard is an astute operator. She's the sort of person whose name appears on lists, with a query against it – customs and excise, police files – but she's slippery and she has extremely good connections. I first ran across her nine or ten years ago, but that was in my professional capacity. One can't help but wonder what she really wanted from Luc Plouviez. Those proposed wedding-bells have a hollow ring for me. The lady is known to have lovers, but this is the first time I've heard of her wanting to marry one of them.'

36

'Could she and Plouviez have been pulling some sort of deal? Maybe he got greedy. Or cold feet.'

'I doubt it. If she were implicated in his death, she'd not have appeared in person at the scene of the crime. Yet she's a very interesting fiancée for any man to have. Also, she'd be an expensive wife. What d'you know about Luc Plouviez?'

'Damn all,' said Durieux crossly. 'I took him at face value, on the say-so of the family. Did he get injured on board ship? It's supposed to have been due to a shell exploding during gunnery practice.'

'I wonder. Plouviez was listed as being on the staff of our naval attaché in Athens. Not a boat in sight, and surely the eastern Mediterranean is no place for gunnery practice, if there was one. But the Greek islands are great jumping-off places for the Lebanon,' said Orloff reflectively. 'On the other hand this may have nothing to do with your case, Inspector.'

'It looked open and shut to me. There isn't a whiff of another suspect or motive. The Foucard woman was still on the road when Plouviez was killed. We've established that.'

'Ah, yes, the petrol pump attendant outside Guingamp, who cast a lascivious eye on her. I know about him.'

'If there's something still to dig out, that woman will know about it,' said Durieux, with conviction. 'If there was a shady deal on, it could be someone was after the pair of them. It'd also explain why Plouviez marooned himself out at Devil's Bay. It's a good place to hide.'

'I appreciate your enthusiasm,' Orloff remarked drily.

'I'd be damned glad to see Christine go free. It's a pity she ever met Luc Plouviez. My guess is, she let herself be persuaded to meet him out of curiosity, took an interest out of compassion for his condition and found herself fatally involved before she knew it. And by then it was too late.' He broke off as a new thought struck him. 'That house is a peculiar choice for a man needing medical attention. It's a long way from anywhere.'

'It belonged to him,' Orloff pointed out.

'He'd paid no attention to it for yonks.'

'Yet he doesn't appear to have considered selling it. Perhaps he'd always had the intention of living in it for his retirement.'

'Rather him than me,' said the Inspector, who lived in a trim modern villa and liked it very much. 'The old uncle who built it was a right eccentric. Could be, it runs in the family. Unless he meant to have a go at finding the old man's treasure, once he was well enough.'

Orloff's eyebrows rose. 'Treasure? In these days?'

Durieux laughed. 'Perhaps he'd never heard of safe deposit boxes. It was one of the old rumours I picked up. I doubt if there's anything in it. Emile Plouviez was supposed to have something valuable hidden in that house. It's the sort of tale that gets invented about characters like that. The woman who kept house for Luc swears there's nowhere to conceal anything. She should know.'

'With the place shut up for many years, have there been break-ins to get at this supposed treasure?'

Durieux shook his head. 'I checked. Nothing ever reported. That kills the treasure rumour for me.'

'Curious,' Orloff commented. 'Now I must make a start. Please advise the prison that I shall be coming to interview Mademoiselle Christine, and then I'll take a look at the scene of the crime. But first' – he placed a large shapely hand on the bulky folder in front of him – 'first, I must digest all this.'

Weary, resigned and not looking for any encouragement, Christine Kergrist followed the wardress into a barely-furnished room for yet another police interview. She was sick of it all, yet wondered what new questions Inspector Durieux had dreamed up this time. Durieux, her enemy now, the man she had called 'Uncle Alain' all her life . . .

It was a shock when a stranger walked in, and once more she was overwhelmed by the fear against which she had fought every moment since her arrest. It was the ongoing nightmare, gazing into a veiled and dark future. Seated on a hard chair on one side of a table, she clasped her hands tightly together in her lap in an effort to regain control.

The stranger took a seat opposite her, snapping his fingers for the wardress to withdraw. She went reluctantly, taking up position on the other side of the door, peering at them through a glass panel.

'Orloff,' he introduced himself. 'I am acquainted with your father.'

She blinked, then gasped. 'I didn't believe you'd come,' she whispered, taking her first good look at him.

'Brigadier Kergrist told you he had been in contact with me?'

She shook her head. 'Not a word. Don't let Papa know. I dragged it out of my mother while he was in Paris. She was worried sick. She was afraid it might lose him his job.'

'And what was your opinion, Mademoiselle?'

'I thought she was right. Policemen aren't supposed to step out of line, are they? Not even' – a sudden lump constricted her throat – 'not even to help a stupid daughter.'

'Don't distress yourself, Mademoiselle. You and your mother had every reason to worry: it was a dangerous thing to do. But no word of that visit will pass my lips. I suggest you and your mother keep silent too. Whatever happens, remember your father's devotion to you. That should sustain you, if I fail to do anything for you.'

Tears came into her eyes. 'I haven't always been a good daughter, not lately.'

A glimmer of a smile appeared. 'You may sort that out with your parents later. For the moment, I'm obliged to ask you a lot of painful questions.'

'I'll tell you everything I know.' A thought struck her, and for a moment she hesitated, then said, 'Marcel Landais would have a fit.'

'Your lawyer, I believe?'

'He's a funny little man, and I think he's on the make for himself rather than me, but I suppose I'm lucky to have him. No one else would care to defend me. Anatole Plouviez has Tremerrec's legal establishment in his pocket. Landais wants to score off him.'

Orloff made a note. 'Anatole? Which one is he?'

'Luc's cousin. Very much the head of the family. You're sure to meet him. A pompous brute.'

'You know the family, of course?'

'I was at school with Sacha, his son. The one who introduced me to Luc,' she added, painfully.

'Sort out these Plouviez for me, please. Where does Anatole fit in?'

'His father was the elder brother of Emile who built that horrible house at Devil's Bay. There was a third brother, the youngest. He was Luc's father.'

The Commissaire picked up the word. 'Was? Luc Plouviez was forty. At that age, his parents could be expected to be living.'

'His mother was older than that when he was born. Luc was an afterthought. He had a brother, Paul, who was twelve years older than he was. Does it matter?'

'I don't know, yet,' Orloff admitted. 'Indulge me. I like to know the background.'

'It can't have anything to do with what happened to Luc. Until a few months ago, he hadn't been back here for twenty years or more,' Christine insisted.

'If you didn't kill him, Mademoiselle, I have to look elsewhere. The family is always top of the list. Who inherits?'

'I've no idea.'

'Then let me work at this my own way. So, we are looking at the descendants of Emile Plouviez and his brothers. Who are they?'

'I only know Anatole and his sister and their children.'

'You mentioned Luc's brother, Paul. What about him?'

'He was drowned. At the same time as Uncle Emile.'

The Commissaire gazed at her. 'No one has mentioned that to me.'

'It was ages ago. I don't know the details. Luc was away at sea, or he might've gone too. It was some sort of general outing. The guy who kept house for Emile was in the boat with them.'

'Did he survive?'

'No. That's why the house was left shut up for all those years. Some people thought it was haunted. It certainly was spooky,' she added reminiscently. 'I suppose all the old wives' tales about it are flying round the district again now.'

'What sort of tales?'

Christine pulled a face. 'The usual rot. Bad luck to anyone who lives there, and so on.'

'Why did Luc suddenly decide to open up the place and live in it?'

'I never asked him. It wouldn't be everyone's choice, but he needed somewhere to live. For convalescence, I suppose it's as good a place as any. That accident made a fearful mess of him.'

'You're studying medicine, I believe? What would be your clinical opinion of his wounds?'

A small weak smile appeared on her face. 'I'm only a beginner, Commissaire.'

'All the more reason for you to be observant. Did you change the dressings for him?'

She nodded, thinking hard. 'He'd lost one leg. He was lucky to have kept the other.' She hesitated, then went on in an uncertain tone, 'You understand, I only saw the end-product of several operations. I'm in no position to criticise the procedures at naval hospitals, and I don't know what state he was in after the accident. Maybe he was trapped in some place where they could stop him bleeding to death but couldn't operate. I think he was left quite a time before receiving proper treatment.'

'Did you ask him?'

'Once, but he shut me up. He didn't want to talk about it. One could hardly blame him.'

'How crippled was he?'

'He could get about, slowly, with a stick. He had an artificial leg, but it wasn't all that comfortable. He made himself wear it. He was determined to live as normal a life as possible.'

'A brave man,' Orloff commented.

A spasm of pain crossed Christine's face. 'Yes, Commissaire. I don't understand why anyone should want to kill him.'

'You know the substance of the charge against you, Mademoiselle: that you did it, in a passion of jealous rage at being jilted.'

'I didn't – ' she burst out fiercely, but was cut short.

'Let's waste no time on protestations. You loved this man. Did you intend to marry him?'

'Yes, I did. I told him I didn't care that he – ' she stopped, biting her lip.

There was a moment's awkward silence, then Orloff said quietly, 'If I am to help you, I must know everything.'

'Does that mean you believe I'm innocent?' she demanded.

'At this stage, I have no opinion. I shan't form one until I'm in possession of all the facts.'

'And then you'll agree with Inspector Durieux and the rest of them,' Christine declared bitterly.

'Would you prefer me to go away?' Orloff enquired.

Eyes blazing with defiance could not meet his cool gaze. 'I'm sorry,' she gulped. 'I'm being stupid.'

'You're under a great deal of strain, Mademoiselle. I think I know what you're holding back. Those injuries Luc sustained were serious. Had they rendered him impotent?'

41

She blushed scarlet. 'He was afraid so.'

'You don't know for sure? Therefore, you were not his mistress?'

The medical student in her surfaced. 'Luc was in no condition to have sexual relations. He was in far too much pain.'

A smile lit up Orloff's face, leaving Christine blinking at the transformation. 'Mademoiselle, I find you refreshing. We're nearly through the worst of it now. When did Marguerite Foucard appear on the scene?'

'He didn't love her. He was using her to drive me away. He knew I'd never agree to leaving him.'

'Is that your own conclusion, or did he tell you?'

'My own conclusion,' she admitted bravely.

'So, we must stick to facts. A romance between a young girl and an older man is nothing new. How far had things progressed between you and Luc Plouviez?'

'I knew I loved him, and I believed that he loved me too. Nothing had been said. He'd never touched me until a few days before that woman turned up. Then, quite unexpectedly, we kissed. I thought I had entered Paradise, but Luc pushed me away, saying he shouldn't have done it. He told me to stay away until I'd thought it all out. He made me promise that I wouldn't come back for at least a week. But before that was up, he wrote to me announcing that Marguerite had arrived and they were going to be married.'

'Giving you no explanation?'

Colour rushed up into her face. 'He said it was a long-standing arrangement. I felt the world had come to an end.'

'At your age, one does,' said Orloff drily. 'What did you do with yourself?'

'Moped about the place, quarrelled with my parents, made myself generally objectionable.'

'You didn't see him?'

'Not until the day of the Pardon at Port Briac.'

'Tell me exactly what you did that day.'

'I went with my parents. I was sitting with the rest of the girls – we have cousins there – but just before the Mass began I felt I had to go and see Luc. I borrowed a bike and cycled over there. It's not very far.'

'To what end?'

Christine shrugged. 'I hadn't thought it out clearly. I'd got over the shock of his letter and it was still firmly fixed in my mind that he truly loved me. I couldn't believe he really wanted to marry that woman. I wanted to see her – to see them together – I thought I'd know, for sure, then.'

'What did you do when you reached Devil's Bay? Did you go straight to the house?'

She shook her head. 'I lost my nerve. I climbed up to The Chasm – it's always fascinated me. And from there you can see over the top of the rocks to the house. It looked deserted and I thought they must have gone away. So I scrambled down for one last look at it. The back door was open. I called, but there was no reply. I went in and found Luc in the living room, lying on his face.' Haunted eyes gazed at Orloff. 'I see him, in my dreams.'

'Did you see anyone in the vicinity of the house before you went in?'

'No, I didn't, Commissaire. I wish I had.'

'At least you've had the sense not to invent anyone. Lies of that sort are generally exposed in court. Go on.'

'At first, I thought he was dead. There was a wound on the back of his head and a poker lying near him, with blood on it. I picked that up to examine it. Then I heard a faint sound from him, so I knelt down beside him, to feel his pulse. He grabbed my hand and held on to it. I think he knew who I was, although his eyes were shut. I dared not move him and I couldn't get my hand free, so I lay down beside him and held him while he died.' She ended on a sob.

Orloff gave her time to recover then said, 'And after that Madame Foucard walked in on you.'

'She was very cool. She didn't have hysterics or anything. She sent for the police.'

'This Pardon at Port Briac,' said Orloff, after a reflective pause. 'You knew you would be going? Or was it a last-minute decision?'

'We always go. My mother's family still live round there. I hadn't thought about going to see Luc, then it occurred to me that I'd have time for a quick visit and be back for the procession before anyone had missed me.'

'You walk in the procession?'

'Ever since I was little.'

Orloff's eyes narrowed. 'In national dress?'

Christine sighed. 'We have things handed down from my great-grandmother. They're ruined now. There's blood on them.'

'I agree you were hardly dressed for committing a murder, Mademoiselle,' the Commissaire remarked drily.

She shuddered. 'They insist I had a sudden impulse in the course of a quarrel and picked up that poker – '

Orloff cut in: 'Let's consider the poker. You must have realised it was a case of murder – no one can batter themselves to death accidentally – and the poker was clearly the weapon. There was plenty of blood on it. Why did you touch it?'

Christine stared at him helplessly. 'I don't know. I didn't think.'

He gazed back at her, coolly assessing. 'That argues for the suspension of reason due to shock, but since you were found with the newly-dead victim, I doubt if it makes much difference. Did you know who Madame Foucard was when she surprised you?'

'No. I wasn't aware she was there until she grabbed me and pulled me away from Luc. She had a grip like steel,' Christine added, feeling her arm reminiscently.

'What did she say to you?'

'I don't remember . . . yes, I do. She said "You've killed him".'

'And what did you reply to that?'

'Nothing, I think. I couldn't take my eyes off Luc. All I knew was that he was dead, the world seemed to have stopped and I didn't care what happened to me.'

'But you do now?'

A flame leapt up in her eyes, then, as quickly, died down. 'I have to, Commissaire. Somehow, I must survive all this. Truly, I didn't kill Luc.'

'Somebody did.'

Christine did not respond. Slowly, dejectedly, she shook her head.

'How much do you know about the twenty-odd years Luc Plouviez spent away from Brittany?'

She looked up, surprised. 'You mean, it could've been someone from his Navy service?'

'My dear young lady, if you didn't kill him, and none of his family appears to have a motive, someone from outside has to be considered,' Orloff rapped out. 'Now then, kindly answer my question.'

'But I can't tell you anything. Luc wasn't the sort of man to spin yarns about where he had been and what he had done. He didn't like me to ask.'

'And you weren't curious? It sounds a bit too perfect to me, Mademoiselle. So does something else. I have just offered you a chance to accuse anyone you choose. Yet you haven't offered me a single name. I find that peculiarly interesting.'

Chapter 4

Inspector Durieux gazed round at the grim scenery of Devil's Bay. In front of him lay the track to the Plouviez house; to one side reared up the broken cliff which concealed The Chasm where the incoming tide boiled and roared; behind him the dry saucer of rock was flooded into a lagoon, and the police drivers waited patiently beside their cars on the causeway. Durieux also waited, while, beside him, the Commissaire stared, registering every detail of the wild bay.

They had met, by arrangement, to inspect the scene of the crime, Orloff coming straight from the prison.

'Where are the girl's clothes?' he demanded suddenly. 'Don't the bloodstains tell us anything?'

The Inspector was unwilling to stick his neck out. The great man would have to see for himself. 'In your office by now, Commissaire,' he replied, warily, wondering what had happened during the interrogation of the girl to arouse in Orloff such patent irritation. 'We'll go back there, if you prefer.'

'No, I want to do this before the light fades,' said the Commissaire, and Durieux resigned himself to going home late.

Orloff's gaze swept over the queer, eroded rocks. 'Why did old Uncle Plouviez build himself a house here?'

The Inspector shrugged. It was all long before his time. 'According to the family, he was eccentric. He wouldn't even have a telephone.'

'Or a car? That track's not wide enough to take one. Is there another entrance?'

'On the far side. But that's no more than a path either. It leads out on to a farm track. I wouldn't care to take a vehicle over this terrain. It's full of boulders. Luc Plouviez hadn't got a car. He used to order a taxi when he needed to go out.'

'How? Or had he installed a telephone?'

'No. He'd send messages by the woman who came in every day. Of course, she wasn't there on August 15th, being a holiday.'

'Then how was the alarm raised by Madame Foucard?'

'She drove to the nearest farm.'

'Leaving Christine Kergrist alone in the house?'

Durieux could see where the Commissaire was heading. 'She had the sense not to bolt. It wouldn't have been difficult for us to pick her up.'

Orloff grunted. 'Would you say that fits in with the picture of a girl suffering a brainstorm and taking a poker to her faithless lover?'

'As, no doubt, the Prosecution will point out. That means: premeditation,' said Durieux gloomily.

'In those clothes? Possibly. And we mustn't rule out sanity returning in a rush the moment the deed was done. But in that case, I would have expected that girl to admit it and throw herself on the mercy of the court, as her lawyer advises.'

There was a short silence, then Durieux exploded: 'There isn't a shred of evidence to give her the benefit of the doubt. Believe me, I looked.'

'I'm not questioning your competence, Inspector. There may be no evidence.' He gazed at the rocky path. 'That's not a good surface for footprints.'

'There'd been a storm, everything was wet. There were traces, but only of the two women,' Durieux reminded him, as if the Commissaire had not read the file thoroughly enough. 'You must have seen the photographs.'

Orloff smiled faintly. 'All that proves is that both of them arrived after the storm. The bicycle tracks you found in the sand at the base of those rocks bear that out. I need to know the exact timing of that storm, which would wash out any tracks made earlier.'

He turned away from the path to the house, gazing up at the mass of worn and jagged rocks which formed The Chasm.

'The girl says she went up there first,' he remarked.

'The place has a fascination,' Durieux acknowledged. 'She left her bike at the bottom.'

They climbed up to stare down the split in the rock, a fissure ever-deepened by the battering of the daily tides. Beyond, along the wide sweep of the bay, a couple walked their dog in the evening light.

'There must have been people about that day. Holiday-makers, picnickers,' said Orloff, eyeing them.

'Plenty, but they scattered when the storm broke.'

'Have you found anyone who saw either of the women?'

Durieux pointed to the far side of the lagoon. 'There's a café of sorts behind that heap of rocks. You can't see it from here. It's a little house backed on to the rocks for shelter, and you can see right across to the causeway from there. The guy in charge of the icecream stall outside saw Christine pedalling up. There was no missing her in her Breton gear.'

'What time was that?'

'Eleven or thereabouts, he thinks. When the rain had stopped.'

'Did he also see Madame Foucard?'

'He says not. Cars began rolling up shortly after he saw Christine and business was brisk.'

'What about the occupants of those cars, and the people who were there before the storm broke?'

Durieux shrugged. 'You know how it is. Folks don't like mixing it with us *flics*. A few came forward, but we got nothing out of them. Not to add to what we knew. After all, we don't have to establish that Christine went to the house.'

'So far, she has proved a most reliable witness,' Orloff remarked.

'No one questions her intelligence, Commissaire. She told it as straight as she dared. Except for what happened at the house,' the Inspector added, conscientiously upholding the official decision of the *juge d'instruction*. 'But it wasn't very bright to leave fingerprints all over the murder weapon.'

'Precisely,' said Orloff.

Durieux shot him a worried glance. 'The evidence is all against her, and there isn't a hint of motive other than jealous rage. She'd even worked out an alibi. She told the child whose bike she borrowed that she'd be back in time for the procession at the Pardon at Port Briac. Then no one would suspect her of having slipped away. With all that crowd at the Mass, no one would notice her absence. It was the storm that ruined the timing. It was only a local one, she couldn't be sure it'd blow across to Port Briac, so she daren't turn up there soaked. She had to shelter till the worst of it was over, and that blew her alibi to bits.'

'Did the storm hit Port Briac?'

'A bit later. It broke up the procession for a while. By that time, her parents had discovered she was missing.'

'Interesting,' Orloff commented, turning away from The Chasm and gazing in the direction of the house. 'From here, Christine went straight to the house? Which way?'

'Across those rocks, to join the path halfway.'

They set off in her footsteps.

'We found imprints of her shoes in pockets of wet sand,' said Durieux. 'Very clear, they were. She was wearing a smart pair of black patents, not usual for scrambling over rocks.'

The house loomed up before them, a tall, stark building of local stone with a grey slate roof. In the centre of the façade a tower rose over the front door, flanked by two pairs of windows. No one had ever done any gardening. Rough grass poked up through the scatter of stones on the landward side, and sprouted unchecked at the foot of the steps to the entrance. Orloff wandered round the side and came, abruptly, out on the rocky shore, with the sea barely a metre below and uncomfortably near. A rusted, weed-encrusted chain dangled from a ring cemented into a large, flattish rock, but the boat it had moored was long gone.

The Commissaire turned away and stopped, his attention caught by a new-looking garden bench beside a flat chunk of concrete serving as a table. He strode over to it.

'What's this?' he enquired. 'It looks like the top of some underground building.'

Durieux joined him. 'It's what's left of a look-out post. They're dotted all round the coast. There'd be machine-guns in it. Hitler's Western Wall. It was dynamited after the war.'

'Not altogether successfully,' Orloff remarked. 'Let's take a look inside the house.'

'The family's agitating for us to release this place to them,' said the Inspector, unlocking the front door.

'Who does it belong to now?'

'There's no joy for Christine in that direction. No one killed Plouviez for his money. It all goes to some seaman's charity. His executor's Anatole Plouviez. He's pressing for access so that he can go through the papers. All the family inherits is the furniture to quarrel over.'

They entered a cool, dark hall. The Inspector threw back the shutters from a window, and a shaft of light fell across an oriental rug on a tiled floor, a heavily-carved teak chest against a wall hung with Chinese silk, writhing with dragons.

'The whole house is like this,' said Durieux. 'I can't stand this stuff, it gives me the creeps. Wait till you see the Japanese armour. We took samples from that rug,' he went on, reverting to his official self. 'Sand from the path. Off one of the women's shoes.'

He was not disposed to linger in the hall, leading the Commissaire quickly into the main living room. This, too, once the shutters were opened, was revealed furnished with exotic oriental pieces, the relics of Emile Plouviez's years in the Far East. At one end was a large open fireplace, laid with logs. Tongs and a shovel rested against ornate firedogs. The poker was missing.

A chalk outline disfigured a worn carpet. Beside it, a straight line showed the position of the weapon, and scattered circles described a pattern of blood spots.

'Christine says she didn't move him, only lay down beside him to comfort him,' said Durieux. 'Madame Foucard found them like that.'

'How long after the girl arrived?'

'Difficult to say. She's hazy. Maybe a quarter of an hour.'

'Why didn't she send for help?'

'She wouldn't leave him while he was still alive. She's a medical student, Commissaire. She knew he couldn't survive an injury like that. The back of the head was bashed in. And once he'd gone, there was no hurry. She says she stayed with him for quite a while.'

Orloff was pacing about the room, taking in everything it contained like a human camera. 'Wasn't this place shut up for twenty years? It all looks to be in remarkably good condition.'

Durieux was not particularly interested. 'The house is dry, although it's almost in the sea. Good solid construction.'

The Commissaire ambled from room to room. At the head of the stairs, on the dim and shuttered landing, he was duly surprised by the four standing suits of black armour, with their grotesque and fearsome facemasks. He ended up in a small room at the top of the tower. It was stacked with boxes.

'What's in those?' he asked, answering his own question as he removed a lid and saw a jumble of papers.

'Family stuff,' said the Inspector. 'We didn't make a thorough search. It's been locked up here since the old man was drowned, I'm told. No one could find the key, and Luc had to force the door. Proper magpie Emile Plouviez was, never threw a thing away.'

Orloff replaced the box. 'It's getting late. I'm keeping you from your family,' he said unexpectedly. 'I'll examine this house in detail tomorrow. Do you set a guard on it?'

'Not since we finished in here,' Durieux replied, astonished and curious. 'No one's tried to break in. D'you want a guard?'

'Until I've completed my own examination, if you please. And would you make an appointment for me with Maître Anatole Plouviez? For first thing in the morning, if possible.'

'Yes, Commissaire. Are you expecting intruders?'

Orloff smiled. 'Merely a precaution, Inspector. My presence here may upset someone. I don't believe in taking unnecessary risks.'

'You think Christine Kergrist is innocent?' Durieux almost shouted.

'I'm keeping an open mind. That's my job.'

'Do you wish to see the girl's parents?'

'I doubt if they can add to their statements,' Orloff replied, slightly offhand. 'I propose to pay a courtesy call at some stage. Brigadier Kergrist is a good officer. It's through no fault of his that his daughter is accused of murder.'

Commissaire Orloff had elected to stay in a hotel in the middle of Tremerrec, on the grounds that most of the possible witnesses were in the town. One of them was seated in the dining room when he entered late that evening. Spotting him, and returning his slight bow with a basilisk stare, Marguerite Foucard looked as though she had just discovered she was drinking from a poisoned chalice. Her companion, a weasely little man with thinning black hair slicked back from a pasty face, looked round. Sharp dark eyes followed the tall police officer's progress to a corner table. Then the pair of them left abruptly.

Orloff witnessed their retreat in some amusement and made a

note of the man's appearance, to be phoned to his office in Paris in the morning. It would be interesting to know which of the woman's associates answered to that description, and even more interesting to know what he did for a living.

He ate at leisure, then went out for a stroll, which brought him in front of the Kergrist house. Encouraged by a light in a ground-floor room, he rang the bell. Bolts rattled, the door opened a crack, then, with an exclamation of surprise from someone on the other side, was flung wide.

'You're here! I can't believe it,' croaked Kergrist, then turned his head to yell upstairs, 'Marie, the Commissaire's here. Come quick.' He became aware, all at once, of two facts: one, that Orloff was still on the doorstep waiting for him to move out of the way; and, two, that he was in his shirtsleeves. 'Excuse me, sir. We were just going up to bed. Please come in.'

'My apologies for arriving so late. I wasn't intending to call tonight but I saw your lights,' Orloff replied, walking into the narrow hall as Marie Kergrist flew down the stairs, buttoning a hastily pulled-on dress. 'Good evening, Madame,' he added, with a smile.

She was overwhelmed by his presence, his size, and the quality of that smile. To the intense embarrassment of her husband, she burst into tears.

'Now, Marie – ' he stuttered.

'Don't keep Monsieur le Commissaire standing in the passage,' she gulped, wiping her eyes. 'I didn't think there'd be anything that you could do for us,' she added, turning to the unexpected visitor and opening the parlour door for him.

'I've no wish to raise false hopes, Madame,' he replied gravely. 'There may be nothing.'

Brigadier Kergrist was setting glasses and a bottle of cognac on the table. 'We know that, Commissaire. The main thing is: you're here. If there's anything that's been overlooked, you'll find it.'

'I hope your confidence isn't misplaced,' said Orloff, to damp overenthusiasm. 'The case against your daughter is strong enough to stand up in court. The main problem for the Prosecution will be Mademoiselle Christine herself. She's impressive.'

'She wouldn't lie,' said Marie simply. 'If she'd killed Luc in a fit of rage, she'd admit it.'

'I believe you, Madame. Unfortunately, that's not hard evidence. You, I understand, are from Port Briac. Tell me what you remember about the Plouviez family. It might help.'

She stared at him helplessly. 'Such as what?'

'I don't know. I'm searching for some little thing which might open up a new angle. The house, for instance. It must have been occupied when you were a girl.'

'I remember it being built, Commissaire. I'd be fourteen or fifteen then, with a pair of long ears to listen to my parents' conversation,' Marie said, with a wan and fleeting smile. 'There was a lot of opposition.'

'It's a monstrosity,' Orloff agreed.

'It spoils the bay. My father tried to put a stop to it being built, but Emile Plouviez had bought the land, and he was willing to tidy up the mess they'd left when they tried to blow up the gun-emplacements.'

'They were big guns? I was told a look-out post with machine-guns.'

Marie shook her head. 'More than that, I think. I can't give you the details. Papa could, if you're interested. He was in the Resistance during the war. A gang of them tried to knock out those guns in advance of D-Day. He and his friend were the only two to survive. They'd been campaigning for a memorial to be put there, to honour the dead. He was furious about the house. But money talked, as usual. That and the Plouviez influence.'

Kergrist shifted his seat uncomfortably. 'Marie, don't!'

She turned on him. 'Why shouldn't I? You know how lawyers stick together. They're as thick as thieves with that *juge d'instruction*.'

'He was only doing his job with the evidence presented to him,' her husband replied doggedly. 'The Plouviez haven't got an axe to grind, except to see someone brought to book. They don't inherit. Luc left all his money to charity.'

'So they pick on the nearest person to satisfy their head-hunting – our Christine.'

Orloff recognised that this was an on-going argument, which was tearing the couple apart. He felt a pang of pity for them. 'Try not to think too much about it, Madame. I assure you that same magistrate would be ready to release Christine if a good case could be made against another party, or even if he were convinced

53

that she was not guilty and the case should be reopened. Tell me about the day that Luc sprang this fiancée on her.'

The Kergrists exchanged glances, then Marie said, 'That was when we finally lost her. Up till then we could talk to each other, even if only by arguing and quarrelling. I was in the kitchen when she walked in, white-faced, and announced that Luc was engaged to that woman. That was all she'd say about it. She spent all her time in her room with her books. She came down to meals when I called her, but she only pecked at the food – '

Kergrist took up the tale. 'She hardly went out, wouldn't even play her discs. I used to complain about those – ' He stopped abruptly, choking back a surge of emotion.

'We didn't know if she'd go with us to the Pardon,' said Marie, 'until I found her ironing her things the night before. Then she told me not to worry, she was over it. But it seemed to me that I was talking to a stranger,' she added desolately.

Orloff did not care for the sound of it. Such unnatural calm might erupt in an explosion . . .

And was it possible that Christine might have suffered a brainstorm but retained no memory of it? He would have to ask the shrinks.

He beat a tactful retreat from the stricken household and walked back to his hotel. As he crossed the square, the carillon rang the hour from the Cathedral spire. Eleven o'clock. It had been a long day . . .

It was not ended for him. As he entered the hotel foyer he saw three people standing at the reception desk. One of them was Marguerite Foucard, but she had new companions: a stocky man with a tinge of grey in his brown hair, and wearing expensive casuals suitable for a humid September evening; the other, clearly newly arrived and booking in, dressed in dark city clothes, tall and slender. Orloff's eyes narrowed. He thought he recognised that elegant back and the black-haired head bent over the register.

Marguerite glanced round and saw him, had a word with the two men, then swept off up the stairs, tossing her head defiantly at Orloff as she went. The stocky man came over to him, hand outstretched.

'Commissaire Orloff? A pleasure to meet you. Anatole Plouviez,' he announced, trying to impress with a firm grip and finding himself outclassed.

At the desk, the other man had received his key and was directing the porter as to the disposal of his baggage. He turned and Orloff perceived that he had made no mistake. It was Bernard de Montigny, expensive legal talent, imported from Paris.

Anatole was introducing them, but the Commissaire interposed quietly, 'Maître de Montigny and I are acquainted.'

Bernard was not much over thirty but making a reputation for himself in the courts, his thin, handsome aristocratic face no disadvantage. He also knew his business.

'I'm representing Madame Foucard's interests,' he said easily, but eyeing the Commissaire with reserve.

'Most interesting,' said Orloff blandly, and Bernard's eyes narrowed.

'My distinguished colleague will be using a room in my office while he's here,' Anatole put in importantly, 'if you wish to see him at any time.'

'I shouldn't think so,' Orloff replied indifferently. 'But you, Monsieur, I do wish to talk to. I had asked Inspector Durieux to fix an appointment with you for tomorrow morning.'

Anatole waved a pudgy hand expansively. 'Any time at your convenience, Commissaire.'

'Would nine thirty be too early?'

'My pleasure, Commissaire. May I offer you a nightcap?'

Orloff hesitated fractionally, then accepted graciously. Bernard de Montigny, with Anatole's hand on his shoulder in an over-familiar fashion, had no choice but to go with them.

The Commissaire wondered how much more brandy he would be obliged to drink that night, and gave silent thanks for a long line of hard-headed ancestors who had kept the Russian winter at bay with many a bottle.

Anatole was in full spate. 'The name of Orloff is known and respected here. It's a great honour to have you, though one wonders that such an insignificant case should interest you.'

Bernard choked slightly at the flat-footed approach, but the Commissaire did not turn a hair.

'The justice of the French Republic reaches both high and low, Monsieur,' he said, deadpan, and Bernard buried his face in his handkerchief again. 'Mine is a routine visit to check on police procedures. The trial is likely to raise a good deal of interest in the gutter press. We don't wish to find ourselves facing an

55

exposé for some minor fault. Nor' – he added, with a sidelong glance at the suffering Parisian lawyer – 'nor do we wish to have details of the private lives of witnesses sprung on us. I am also here to collect background information.'

'You shall have my full cooperation,' Anatole declared. 'My family has nothing to hide. But I take your point about the popular press, Commissaire. Those fellows don't care what they say about anyone.'

'Forewarned is forearmed,' Orloff agreed, almost as pompously. 'Luc Plouviez is the sort of figure to attract speculation: a bachelor recluse, crippled in an explosion, torn between a lovely young girl and a handsome woman-of-the-world. It has the ingredients.'

Anatole glanced down into his glass, as if the brandy were the source of the bad taste which, on an instant, had come into his mouth. He decided he had been given enough horrors to go on with.

'If you will excuse me, Commissaire, it's time I went home,' he said, rising. 'I shall look forward to meeting you again tomorrow morning.'

With a bow and a handshake he left. As soon as he had gone, Orloff turned to his remaining companion.

'Why are you staying in the hotel, Monsieur, when your family lives just across the river? Have you quarrelled with them?'

Bernard de Montigny took a sip from his glass. 'By no means, Commissaire. This is business. I wouldn't care to burden the old people. I can deal with things much better from here.'

'Ah, you mean your redoubtable aunt wouldn't appreciate having either Anatole Plouviez or your client on visiting terms.'

'No,' Bernard agreed coolly, hiding grim amusement at the accurate assessment of the situation. He shot a baffled glance at Orloff. He had not anticipated finding it quite so difficult to strike the right note with a man whom he suspected of having been his mother's lover – and who, for all he knew, still was.

'Have you acted for Madame Foucard for long, Maître?'

Bernard breathed a little more freely. Clearly the Commissaire intended to keep their relationship on a formal level. He studied his companion's impassive face, noticing for the first time, a hint of an oriental fold at the corner of each eye. Was the man descended from Tartar princes? He wouldn't be at all surprised.

'Over the past four or five years,' he replied. 'I'm here to protect her from your persecution. Her words, Commissaire. You make her nervous. Are you really here on a routine check on police procedures?'

Orloff smiled. 'Now, you wouldn't expect me to answer that, would you?'

'Try this one: what have you got against my client?'

'Nothing in particular, Maître. Her name crops up from time to time.'

Bernard scented danger and, with lawyer's prudence, began to distance himself from it. 'I handled the purchase of her house in St Cloud and certain items of business since. Her former husband was very generous. Madame Foucard possesses a lot of property which brings in a sizeable income. I have no knowledge of any illegal activities.'

'Then you've nothing to worry about. I'm glad to see you. Perhaps you can persuade Madame Foucard that it might be in her interest to talk to me.'

'Give me one good reason.'

Orloff drained his glass and stood up. 'Oh, my dear sir, tell her to think of the scandal. The gutter press will find your client an even more interesting subject than her late fiancé. I wish you goodnight.'

Thoughtfully, Bernard de Montigny gazed at his retreating back. He had a nasty feeling at being in over his head already. Previous experience of the Commissaire had taught him to be wary. One never knew exactly where Orloff was aiming.

Chapter 5

Marcel Landais was at the prison early the next morning. He cast a sharp eye over his client as she was brought into the interview room, perceiving a subtle change for which he was at a loss to account.

'I have to warn you, Mademoiselle, to expect further police interrogation. Commissaire Orloff is reviewing the case. He has a great reputation. You'll find him formidable,' he added, balefully.

'He was here yesterday evening.'

'So soon?' He wondered if it were the unexpected visitation which had changed her stance. She seemed – he groped mentally for the word – tranquil. 'What did he say to you?'

'He went over my evidence. To hear it for himself, he said,' Christine replied calmly.

Now he was certain of the change in her, and set himself to puncture false hopes. 'Orloff's a busy man. He'll be here for no more than a day or two. Just to check that everything's in order. Cases like yours make the police nervous. The popular papers love a *crime passionnel*,' he said, unable to disguise his own relish. 'It's time you adopted a sensible attitude to your predicament.'

'I'm not prepared to admit to a crime I didn't commit,' she replied, bolstered by her new confidence.

'It's your best bet, Mademoiselle. Anatole Plouviez wants to see you put away for a long stretch. By sticking to claims of innocence in the face of all the evidence, you're trying to take on the legal Establishment. You're bound to lose.'

Christine was willing to put up a fight. 'I don't see that it makes any difference. Your way lands me in prison, too.'

'But not for so long a time,' he replied earnestly. 'As it is, you face a charge of wilful murder, a premeditated crime, accompanied by a sketchy alibi.'

She bit her lip. 'How many times do I have to explain that slipping away from the Pardon was a spur-of-the-moment decision? All I wanted to do was see Luc and Marguerite together for a moment. I had every intention of being back at Port Briac for the procession.'

'It doesn't look that way to the *juge d'instruction*. He thinks it was a clever little alibi, which was ruined by the storm. You haven't anything to offer by way of a defence except your own assertion of innocence. Make no mistake, Mademoiselle, no court is going to accept that. You'll be written down as a bitter, vengeful young woman.'

'And your way I shan't?'

Landais considered he was gaining the upper hand. 'By no means. Please understand that we have no evidence to offer against the charge except your youth and beauty. The defence I propose is that you have told the truth strictly as you know it, but that, in the emotion of the moment, you suffered a brainstorm during which you killed him, and which produced a lapse of memory. You will admit that the evidence shows you killed him, although you can't remember doing it, and you will say you are stricken with grief and remorse, and throw yourself on the mercy of the court. Believe me, Mademoiselle, the eyes of all France, of all Europe, will be on you. Everyone will be sorry for you. Even the judge.'

Christine stared at him. 'All eyes will be on you, too, Monsieur.'

'To our mutual benefit,' he agreed with a smile. 'You should receive a light sentence.'

'For something I didn't do.'

Landais wagged his finger at her. 'Can you really be sure that you didn't have a blackout and not remember anything about it afterwards?'

'I haven't any blanks in my memory,' Christine replied firmly. 'It's all too clear.'

'Then we must fall back on my original line of defence, which, I agree, is better. Pleading amnesia is always risky. I can't present you to the court as a simple country girl. You're a highly intelligent young woman. For your own best interest you must drop this insistence on innocence.'

'Doesn't it matter that the real killer is going to get away with it?' she burst out.

'That's not my business. There's no other suspect except yourself. I would advise you to follow my original advice and plead guilty. Leave me to make the most of your circumstances.' In his mind's eye he could see it all . . . And after his performance in court, Anatole Plouviez and his snooty friends would be obliged to cede to him his rightful place in Tremerrec legal circles. 'A man torn between love of money and love of a beautiful girl.'

Christine winced. 'Luc wasn't like that.'

'He jilted you, didn't he? La Foucard is rich, but she's hardly in her first youth. My guess is she's at least ten years older than your Luc. And shop-soiled. You and she make a fine contrast. To your advantage, Mademoiselle,' he added with a winning smile which brought no response from his client.

Commissaire Orloff was installed in a comfortable chair in Maître Plouviez's office. He appreciated the décor, a combination of unostentatious luxury, old furniture, and shelf upon shelf of hefty tomes, the whole creating an impression of solid tradition. The lawyer had come a long way from the poor fisherfolk of Port Briac who were his ancestors.

Orloff wondered how much the man was irritated by the inevitable dredging-up of family history as a result of the tragedy at Devil's Bay. Plouviez showed no signs of annoyance. On the contrary, he appeared to be enjoying the presence of a more senior police officer than Tremerrec could produce. But was that putting on a good face or an exercise in personal aggrandisement? The Commissaire encountered self-important people on many occasions, and some emerged a little bruised. But not this time: Orloff was intending to ask some highly impertinent questions, and needed the man's goodwill.

'The Defence is going to make the most of the way the girl was jilted,' he remarked, once the official politenesses were over.

From the depths of an even more comfortable chair on the other side of a massive desk, Anatole Plouviez permitted himself a small, satisfied smile. 'They have to, don't they? Not that they've a leg to stand on, even so.'

'Luc Plouviez's name will be blackened. Is that just deserts?'

'I really can't say, Commissaire. Luc was an unsociable fellow. Not like his brother, Paul, who was my best friend.'

'Lost at sea, I'm told.'

Anatole shook his head over an old tragedy. 'A very sad occurrence, Commissaire. We lost Uncle Emile, Paul, and Emile's man, Lim, all in one go. Our coast is dangerous, you understand. Luc lost more than his brother. Their mother never recovered from the shock. She died a few months later, and his father the following year.'

'Is that why Luc never came home during his service in the Navy?'

Plouviez shrugged. 'We supposed so. Until last winter, we hadn't seen him since his father's funeral.'

'What about the house he'd inherited?'

'He couldn't have lived in it even if he'd wanted to. His mother put all the furniture into store, and had the windows boarded up. Since her death, I've had the place inspected once a year. Fortunately for Luc, it's well built, there's been little need for repairs.'

'There was no question of selling the house?' Orloff enquired.

'It wouldn't be everyone's choice, but the situation's magnificent. As a summer residence, it'd be delightful. I wrote to Luc about it once – there was an offer – but he replied that he'd reopen it when he retired. Eccentric, *hein*? In the event, he left the Navy sooner than he expected. He's lived in that place like a recluse since he came home.'

'Did you see him frequently?'

Anatole's mouth turned down in a wry smile. 'I told you, Commissaire, he didn't socialise. Nor did he wish to have anything much to do with the rest of us.'

'Yet Christine Kergrist states she was introduced to him by your son. How did that come about?'

'Not with my approval,' Anatole replied grimly. 'I don't know what's the matter with young people these days. They go out of their way to give pain to their parents.'

'Youth has always rebelled,' said Orloff, with intent to provoke.

'I don't think our generation behaved so outrageously, Commissaire. We had some respect, I recall. Now they go looking for bad company. Not that I had anything against Christine,' he added, hastily, determined to maintain a fair-minded pose. 'She'd have been a good enough girl if she hadn't had ambitions. Her place was in a shop, or perhaps behind a typewriter, but not this nonsense of becoming a doctor. In my opinion, she found herself out of her depth in the university and latched on to poor Luc as a surer way of bettering herself. So you see, her disappointment at being sent packing had rather more of an edge to it than merely being crossed in love.'

'You feel strongly, Monsieur.'

'I make no secret of my bias, Commissaire,' Anatole replied bleakly. 'Luc was a member of my family, and I'm eager to see his murderer brought to justice. Nor can I pretend sorrow that Sacha has had his eyes opened. Even he can't go on mooning after a convicted killer.'

'I appreciate your frankness,' said Orloff encouragingly. 'Your son has a *tendresse* for the girl?'

'Puppy love.' The parent dismissed the matter. 'What more can I do for you, Commissaire?'

'For the moment, nothing, Monsieur. Thank you for your cooperation.'

Anatole came round the desk to usher out his distinguished visitor. 'My pleasure, I assure you. Any time, Commissaire. I'm as anxious as you that this business should be settled without any undue fuss. Does Christine still maintain she's innocent?'

'So far,' Orloff agreed.

'She must be more stupid than I thought. That attitude won't help her in court.'

'I understood you wanted her put away for life, Monsieur.'

Anatole waved a fat hand adorned with a flashy gold ring in which was set a small coin. 'I'm not entirely without heart. A plea of guilty with, perhaps, diminished responsibility, would satisfy me as long as the trial was short and not of lasting interest to the gutter press. We'll have to pin our hopes on Landais. I can't say I appreciate his methods, but if anyone can persuade her to see sense, he's the man.'

In a small room further down the corridor, Bernard de Montigny confronted his client. Clad in an orange and black creation, Madame Foucard was circling the walls in a fair imitation of a caged tiger.

'Why did you have to take this room?' she demanded.

'The offer of it was a courtesy,' he replied coldly. 'It would have been offensive to refuse it. What's more, we have privacy unobtainable at the hotel.'

The elegant shoulders moved in a cross between a shrug and an expression of petulance. 'I fail to appreciate that.'

'It's not my habit to interview clients in a bedroom, Madame,' said Bernard, who was wishing himself back in Paris. Perhaps he should have asked Aunt Lottie . . . but no, that might have made matters worse. 'I was under the impression that you and Maître Plouviez shared a common interest in seeing Luc avenged.'

Marguerite Foucard's generous mouth tightened. 'That, of course. But I don't like being beholden to that man. He can't keep his hands to himself.'

Bernard suppressed a grin. 'I'm sure you're skilled at repelling over-ardent admirers, Madame.'

She cast him a speaking look and turned away to a side table to examine a fine blue-and-white jar which had caught her eye.

'After all, it's a nice little room, with some good pieces in it,' he remarked, gazing round at the appointments of what was generally in use as a waiting room for clients.

Marguerite snorted. 'I've no intention of spending a moment longer than necessary in this place. Let's get down to business. Monsieur. What do you propose to do about Orloff?'

'If I'm to be of any service to you, Madame, I need to know why you claim the Commissaire is persecuting you,' Bernard replied. 'You were vague on the point when you telephoned me.'

She sat down opposite him, still clutching the jar. 'I've a wide circle of acquaintances; perhaps some have been so unlucky as to attract the attention of the *police judiciare*. I can't take any responsibility for them.'

Bernard felt it to be an inadequate explanation. But it was his job to look after her interests, and no lawyer could afford to act solely for the blameless.

'The Commissaire's looking to you to tell him about Luc Plouviez, who's something of a mystery man.'

'I can't see why. The girl's guilt is obvious.'

'Orloff's presence here suggests some doubts. I regret, Madame, but it appears that *you* are the magnet which has drawn him to Tremerrec.'

'I told you: persecution.'

'If I'm to help you, you'd be well advised to tell me what it is that Orloff holds against you,' he said patiently. 'Better still, tell him what he wants to know about Luc,' he added, as she shook her head stubbornly.

'All this fuss over a little bitch who lost her temper,' Marguerite muttered. 'Luc didn't know any of my friends.'

'Then how did you meet him? At the house of a mutual acquaintance is a common situation.'

'Not this time,' she said swiftly. 'It was quite by chance. You might say we were thrown together,' she added, with the hint of a private smile. 'Why all this interest in how I met Luc?'

'The Commissaire seems to think it important. Madame, I am powerless to help you if you will not give me all the facts I need to know. Is there some mystery about Luc Plouviez?'

'How should I know?' she replied indifferently, replacing the pottery jar on its table and making for the door. 'You may tell Orloff that I met Luc at a – what shall I call it? – a party, which neither of us would have chosen to attend. I was distressed at his accident. I looked him up when he was out of hospital, and we discovered we were in love. Will that do?'

Bernard de Montigny was baffled. He was aware of having gone wrong somewhere along the line. Whatever had bothered his client seemed to be troubling her no more.

Commissaire Maximilien Orloff returned to the stark, lonely house at Devil's Bay. There were people on the beach, and the café was doing a lively trade in ice cream. But the police cordon round the property and the bored guard at the mouth of the track kept the curious away. Already the crime had faded from public memory, superseded by greater horrors. Only the trial would bring back spectators to gawp at the scene.

Alain Durieux, in charge of the keys, kept him waiting. Orloff wandered round the side of the house, where a broken wall, partially repaired in recent weeks, marked the boundary of the property. An apologetic and rushed Inspector found him at the back of the house, minutely examining the old mooring ring hammered into a rock.

'Take a look at this,' said Orloff, cutting short the stream of apologies.

Durieux squatted down beside him, following a long finger pointing to a light shred caught in the dark weed round the rusty chain dangling from the ring.

'Rope?' he suggested.

'From some craft which has tied up here,' the Commissaire agreed. 'Fairly recently, too. Is the photographer here? Good,' he went on as the Inspector nodded. 'Get him down here. I want this whole area combed for any other traces of that boat.'

'It might have belonged to sightseers,' Durieux pointed out. 'We don't know how long that bit's been there. I'm afraid I slipped up there. If there were footprints, I missed them.'

'Don't take it to heart. We all make mistakes. In any case, there may not have been any. If that shred of rope is significant, the boat and whoever was in it could have been gone before the storm broke.'

Durieux sat back on his heels. 'I wonder how long Luc Plouviez took to die? The pathologist wouldn't commit himself.'

'If we're to believe Christine, he was unconscious when she found him, shortly after the storm,' Orloff pointed out. 'When did that storm start?'

The Inspector pulled out his notebook, glad to have some information to hand. 'It was localised, hitting this place about ten thirty a.m. It lasted at least a quarter of an hour. From here it passed slowly along the coast, reaching Port Briac shortly before twelve. So we can start constructing a timetable. We know the Mass of the Pardon began at half past ten, more or less. People, including the Kergrist family, began arriving from ten o'clock onwards. Christine borrowed the bike just before the service began and pedalled over to Devil's Bay – '

'How long would that take?'

'Not more than a quarter of an hour or twenty minutes.'

'Right. There was ample time for her to be there and back before half past eleven when the procession was due to move off,' said Orloff. 'But somewhere along the way she had to take shelter from the storm, which adds a minimum of ten minutes to the ride. That confirms eleven for her arrival at Devil's Bay. Then add a few more minutes for lingering at The Chasm. From up there, I wonder if she would have seen a boat tied up at the back of the house?' he added, glancing up at the bare and forbidding rock outcrop.

'If there was one,' said the Inspector. 'Sir, are you convinced of her innocence?'

'Not yet. I'm merely examining the possibilities.'

'The tide would have to be in to tie up here,' Durieux pointed out, gloomily envisaging a hopeless search for a small boat out on a national holiday.

'So check the tide on 15th August last, just to see if it's feasible for a boat to have come in this far that morning.' He gazed down at the water lapping the foot of the rock. 'One could bring in a shallow-draught craft now. Check with your witnesses who were on the beach. Someone may have seen a boat.'

'Dozens, Commissaire. Have you any idea how many small craft there are round this coast?'

'I'm not totally unreasonable, Inspector. It's only on the off-chance. Let's go inside and see what else, if anything, the house has to tell us,' said Orloff, smiling, and Durieux heard himself agreeing eagerly.

'Where did Christine get in?' the Commissaire asked, as the Inspector unlocked the front door.

'She found the kitchen door open. That's round the other side.'

'Away from the beach? Our boatman – if he existed – would not have been seen entering or leaving by that way. How did Madame Foucard get in?'

'She had a key to this door,' said Durieux, standing aside for the Commissaire to enter the house.

'Let me see this kitchen.'

Durieux led him across the hall into a large oblong room. He hastened to pull back the shutters. Orloff stared round at an old-style kitchen. Heavy cupboards stood round the walls; a large scrubbed table filled the centre; and the most arresting features were a huge and ancient range and a sink dominated by a black iron pump.

'Period piece, *hein*?' said Durieux with a grin. 'My wife'd have a fit.'

The Commissaire fancied himself as a cook. 'What sort of water supply is there? That pump must bring up brine,' he said distastefully.

'It's for rainwater. There's a cistern in the roof to collect it. There's a freshwater spring on the edge of the property, on the side towards the farm. It's piped up to the house from there.'

Orloff returned to business. He consulted his notes. 'I see you found sand and cement dust on the floor here.'

'The sand was off the girl's shoes, the cement seems to have been walked in by Luc himself. He'd started repairing the boundary wall.'

'Was he fit enough?'

'He was only doing a bit at a time. A very determined sort of fellow, by all accounts. Those are his tools, just as he left them.'

The Commissaire stepped over to the corner by the back door. Propped against the wall was a spade and a crowbar, both whitened with cement, and on the floor a chisel and a trowel. He examined them briefly, then turned away.

'Fingerprints in this house?'

'Only what one would expect: those of the victim, the two women and the housekeeper. That one, Janine, is a dedicated cleaner,' said the Inspector with a certain regret. 'This place was like a new pin. All we found on the hall floor was a bit of sand from La Foucard's feet. We vacuumed every floor, of course,' he added, as Orloff wandered into the hall.

'And elsewhere?'

'Neither of the women went upstairs after the finding of the body, Commissaire. Luc had wiped his feet in the kitchen – that woman had him housetrained – but there were still traces of cement dust on the soles of his shoes. As I reconstructed it, he'd been working on his wall until the rain started, then came into the house and met his end.'

'On sticks and with a false leg he'd hardly have made a run for it.'

Durieux frowned. 'That doesn't alter anything. He'd see the storm coming and make for shelter in good time. He was a seaman.'

Orloff prowled round the hall, glancing through the open door to the living room, then circling back to the table in the centre. 'I'm told everything was put into store when the house was closed up.'

'That's right,' Durieux confirmed. 'I reckon that's why there weren't any break-ins. Nothing worth stealing.'

'There's plenty of that now, Inspector. Here's your old man's fabled treasure. In every room. Have you any idea what the contents of this house are worth?'

'What, this old stuff?'

'Billions of francs,' said the Commissaire. He picked up a blue pottery bowl ornamented with an irregular pattern of white blossom. 'Unless I'm mistaken, this is K'ang Hsi, three hundred years old. It's a pity its base is missing but, even so, a valuable collector's piece. That armour you dislike so much would fetch a bomb at auction. And the carpet from which you have clipped off blood-spotted pile was made in Isfahan when *le Roi Soleil* was King of France.'

'Good God!' Durieux exclaimed.

Orloff laughed. 'Don't worry, Inspector. Justice has to be served first, and is no respecter of antiques.'

'I was thinking: the family inherits all this.'

'So they do. It opens up an interesting possibility.'

'They're rich people, Commissaire.'

'What's that to do with it? Those with much often want a whole lot more. We must have a valuer look at this place,' Orloff went on briskly. 'And I want a list of all the beneficiaries, as well as an account of where each one was on the day of the murder.'

Durieux was making notes. 'I shouldn't have overlooked this,' he muttered. 'The *juge d'instruction* – ' he broke off.

'Leave him to me, Inspector. The circumstances of this crime were such that it was easy to leap to conclusions. I have an appointment with him this afternoon. I shall tell him my initial enquiries leave me dissatisfied on certain points, and I wish to continue investigating. He won't object.'

Durieux did not doubt it for one moment. If the Commissaire said the case was to be reopened, no local magistrate would stand against him.

'Jules Kergrist will thank you on his knees.'

Orloff shook his head. 'That would be premature. Remember, the obvious isn't necessarily wrong. But there are no short-cuts in a case of murder. Every angle must be explored.'

A gendarme appeared. 'Excuse me, Commissaire. The house-keeper's here.'

'Good,' said Durieux. 'I asked Madame Basret to come, Commissaire. She lives across at the farm.'

Orloff nodded. 'Bring her into the living room, please.'

She was a short, stout woman of late middle age. No one could call her a beauty, and she made no concessions to modern fashions in make-up or dress. With her dark skirt and white blouse, with grey-streaked hair scraped up into a bun on the top of her head, she looked timeless, the archetype peasant. She advanced into the room, her eyes fixed suspiciously on the stranger from Paris.

'Madame,' said the Commissaire, introducing himself. 'Please take a seat.'

Out of the variety of comfortable chairs, she selected a hard upright one, against a wall. Orloff sat himself at her late employer's desk, under a nearby window.

'Just a few questions,' he said easily.

'I've already told him' – she jerked her head in the direction of the Inspector – 'everything I know. I wasn't here the day Monsieur Plouviez was killed.'

Orloff smiled at her. 'I've read your statement. I'm sure it was as complete as you could make it, Madame. I'm not proposing to go over it. I would like you to tell me what sort of man was Luc Plouviez. You must have known him as well as anyone.'

Janine Basret stared at him uncertainly. 'He wasn't much trouble,' she offered.

'A good employer, in fact?'

Still a shade suspicious, she agreed.

'You liked working here?' Orloff went on.

'It suited me,' she admitted, then, encouraged by another smile, burst out: 'It was a Godsend, Monsieur. My son's good to me and his wife's a decent enough girl, but the farm's theirs since I lost my husband. They do their best to make me feel comfortable, but it's not the same.'

Out of her line of vision, the Inspector permitted himself a small grin. He had come to the conclusion that Orloff could charm the birds off the trees, if he chose, and Durieux felt he was witnessing a prime example of the art. For him, getting any sort of a statement out of the housekeeper had been like extracting teeth.

'So you are distressed that your employer is dead, Madame?' the Commissaire was saying smoothly.

'Not only for myself, Monsieur,' she replied swiftly. 'Luc Plouviez was a good man. It was bad enough that he was crippled, but then to be killed like that, and by – ' she broke off, her mouth tightening.

'What did you think of Christine Kergrist?'

'I was never more shocked in my life, when they told me what she'd done. It didn't seem possible. She'd been good for him, given him back the will to live.'

'Yet it seems he preferred Madame Foucard,' Orloff observed.

Janine Basret's eyes flashed fire. 'That one should have stayed in Paris, or wherever she came from. He wasn't best pleased the first time *she* turned up. Monsieur Luc wasn't a man to show his feelings, but I could tell.'

'She arrived unannounced?'

'Out of the blue, Monsieur. Christine wasn't there that day.' She hesitated, frowning. 'It was that woman who caused all the trouble. Christine didn't come again. It's my opinion that painted hussy made him give up the girl.'

'Are you suggesting that Madame Foucard had some sort of hold over Luc Plouviez?'

She shrugged. 'A man of his age, who's been all over the world, is sure to have had a few *affaires*, isn't he? Chickens come home to roost sometimes,' she added, darkly.

'Was he happy in his engagement?'

'Monsieur Luc was too much of a gentleman to wear his heart on his sleeve, but he couldn't fool me. He thought he was doing the "right thing", as if that ever made anyone happy,' Janine declared and burst into tears.

Chapter 6

'It'd have to be a serious *liaison* to make a man go so far as to propose marriage,' muttered Alain Durieux in a disgruntled tone.

The housekeeper had gone, proof against all persuasion to air further opinions after that one outburst against Marguerite Foucard. They were back to the examination of the scene of the crime and the Commissaire was wandering round the room with a scowl on his face.

'An unlikely sort of match,' he agreed. 'I'd thought La Foucard's heart was more in the nature of a cash register. One can't perceive what financial advantage our gallant sailor could bring her.'

'She doesn't look the motherly type, to take on a cripple out of pity,' the Inspector agreed.

'As Maître Landais will make much of, in court,' Orloff remarked sourly. 'How do you reconstruct this crime?'

'The victim was walking away from the fireplace,' Durieux responded, glad to get back to facts. 'The murderer was behind him, having snatched up the poker. Hit him on the head. Straightforward.'

'As far as it goes. It indicates someone known to the victim, admitted by him, an entirely unsuspected source of danger.'

'Which fits Christine Kergrist like a glove,' the Inspector sighed.

'So where was Luc Plouviez going?'

Durieux's eyes snapped wide open. 'Going?'

'Why did he turn his back?'

'In the course of a quarrel?'

'Perhaps. But if the poker was snatched up, surely he would have heard something, enough to make him suspicious if, in fact, a furious quarrel was going on. And consider this,' Orloff invited.

'A quarrel which ends in unpremeditated homicide doesn't happen all of an instant. In my experience, a room gets into a certain amount of disorder in the course of such a quarrel, and neither party turns his back on the other unless to escape through the nearest door.'

'Agreed, but – ' the Inspector broke off, frowning. 'No quarrel?'

Orloff shook his head. 'Not as I read the evidence. Luc was moving away from the fireplace, but not in the direction of the door. He was heading for the opposite side of this room, peaceably, unsuspecting, and if he heard the poker lifted, he had no premonition of danger.'

'That implies premeditation.'

'Without a shadow of a doubt.' Orloff's eyes appraised the furniture over that side of the room. Discounting armchairs, there remained the desk and a sideboard bearing a bottle of cognac and glasses. 'What prints did you lift off those?'

'None but those of Luc Plouviez and the housekeeper from the bottle. The glasses were clean and polished. Basret keeps them that way,' said the Inspector, then added, 'None of this clears Christine.'

'I'm aiming to find the truth. Nothing more. Nothing less. So far, there's not a shred of evidence to contradict the case against that young woman. But neither is there anything much to support it.'

'Only a motive as big as a house,' Durieux objected. 'And her fingerprints on the murder weapon.'

'In a state of shock, an innocent person may handle such an object. What other prints were on that poker?'

'None.'

'I would've expected at least a finger and thumb from the housekeeper when she replaced it after the last time she cleaned it. It's arguable that such a dedicated woman might wipe it over again, but equally it could mean that the murderer cleaned off his own traces. Christine admits that she handled it. The whole case at the moment will turn on whom the court believes.'

'But we hadn't got another suspect, Commissaire.'

'Not yet. There are still areas of intense obscurity. Who knows what they will yield?'

* * *

72

Marie Kergrist was surprised to find Janine Basret on her door-step, the old bicycle on which she trundled laboriously into market every Friday propped against a wall.

But it was not market day, and Marie could not remember when she had received a visit from Janine. She hesitated over asking her in. Since Christine's arrest the Kergrists had shunned society, as their friends drew away from them.

Janine was not one to waste words, especially on the daughter of a neighbouring farm. 'Can we talk?'

Marie fell back. 'You'd better come in.'

She led her into the parlour, stuffy and smelling of polish, not a friendly welcome to a woman she had known all her life. They sat stiffly on opposite sides of the table.

'What's that Commissaire doing here?' Janine said abruptly.

'It's no use asking me,' Marie replied with a stony face.

She and Jules felt embattled, with the whole town, the whole countryside thinking their precious only child a murderess. Already she was regretting letting one of the enemy into the house.

There was a long moment of difficult silence.

Janine drew a deep breath. 'Is there a doubt about who did it?'

'*I've* never doubted Christine's innocence,' Marie hissed back.

Her visitor clasped her workworn hands together and stared down at them. 'Everyone's satisfied she did it.'

'Does that make a lie true, that it's believed?'

'There doesn't seem to be anyone else.'

'There has to be,' Marie declared passionately. 'I know my daughter. What have you come here for?'

Janine took her time in replying. 'I didn't approve,' she said at last. 'The differences were too great between them, but she brought him back to life.'

'Yet you insist she killed him?' Marie snapped back, exasperated.

Slowly, Janine shook her head. 'I believed what I was told. Now I don't know.'

'And you think I can tell you? No matter what they do to Christine, I'll never believe she killed him, even if she did love him too much and he treated her like dirt.'

'He didn't!' Janine flared. 'Monsieur Luc was a true gentleman.'

'True gentlemen don't lead impressionable girls on and then fling them aside when they've had enough of them.'

'It wasn't like that, Marie. He didn't want to send Christine away. That last couple of weeks, when she wasn't there, he was like a lost soul. It was all that woman's doing.'

'Madame Foucard?'

'That *putain*! Men are fools. They make idle promises they don't expect to have to fulfil,' Janine added cryptically.

'Could she have killed him?'

An expression of deep regret passed over Janine's face. 'She was driving from Paris. Or so she says. The police seem convinced.'

Marie sighed. 'I wasn't thinking. Madame Foucard hadn't any reason. She'd got what she wanted. But she's a stranger. It'd be a relief to blame her. There has to be someone else. Who came to the house?'

'Hardly anyone. The doctor now and then.'

'And Christine every day,' said Marie in a deadly voice.

'There's no getting away from it, not that I blame you for defending your child.'

'Ah, but Commissaire Orloff's here now. Whatever else is there, he'll find it.'

All colour drained from Janine's face. 'How can you be so sure?' she demanded harshly. 'I'd better be going. I'm late.'

On the steps, she all but collided with the Brigadier, returning home for his dinner. The sight of the police uniform sent Janine and her bicycle wobbling dangerously down the steep street.

'That was Janine Basret, surely?' he exclaimed, staring after her, amazed that she reached the bend in the road without mishap. 'What was she doing here?'

'I don't know,' his wife admitted. 'She said she wanted to talk. Something's happening, Jules.'

He kissed her cheek. 'I expect the Commissaire is stirring the pot. Don't build too many hopes on it, yet, *chérie*.'

Marie served the food with a preoccupied air, then sat down to do no more than pick at her plate. Presently, she looked up. 'I think Janine wants to believe Christine did it, in spite of detesting the Foucard woman. Why should she? What's Christine done to her?'

Kergrist chewed thoughtfully. 'I'd say she was worried about Pierre.'

74

'Him? I thought he was in prison somewhere?'

'That's right. In England. He might be out by now. Pierre's Janine's youngest and her favourite by a long chalk. In her shoes, I'd be worried. That *sale type* won't be going straight, whatever he's doing. If he's in Brittany and Orloff sends out the dragnet for all the bad boys, he could be back inside before he can look round.'

'He's not likely to have killed Luc Plouviez,' Marie said, impatiently. 'The more's the pity!'

Inspector Durieux popped his head round the door to Commissaire Orloff's temporary office, enquiring if the great man required anything more. It was unlikely, since all exhibits of physical evidence in connection with the murder of Luc Plouviez had been assembled for his inspection, save for the corpse itself. Orloff was surrounded by items neatly tied in plastic bags and labelled. Spread out on the desk were the clothes worn by both victim and accused.

The Commissaire glanced up from brooding over them and invited him in. 'Everything here confirms the girl's story. Equally, it suggests her guilt. Take your pick which to believe. Yet there are a couple of points which, to me, are unexplained,' he added, and lapsed into some sort of meditation.

'Such as?' Durieux prompted him.

'One: why did she remain with the corpse if she killed him?'

'To make sure he really was dead and couldn't betray her?'

'Another wop on the head would've ensured that,' Orloff pointed out. 'My second objection is more concrete. It concerns the shoes.'

The Inspector brightened, reassured by the return to solid evidence. 'What about them?'

The Commissaire picked up a smart black patent leather pump. 'Christine was wearing this. Now, we know she had been in the churchyard at Port Briac, but the ground there was dry at the time she left, so there'd be nothing more than a little dust on the shoes.' He consulted the laboratory report. 'Duly noted here. She sheltered during the storm, collecting a small amount of different dust, then climbed up to The Chasm and from there made her way to the house, collecting wet sand. She entered by the kitchen door and wiped her feet on a mat. According to existing evidence, no one else used that entrance that morning. When was the house cleaned last?'

'The day before the holiday. The Basret woman's houseproud. She doesn't leave a speck anywhere, polishes everything in sight, including the *patron*'s shoes, would you believe?' said Durieux, with a grin. 'She did the kitchen last, just before she left. Useful, *hein*?'

'Very,' Orloff agreed. 'It gives us purer samples, although the kitchen doormat was sure to have received thousands of particles and retained a good many of them.'

'We only took off the top layer, Commissaire.'

'Well done, Inspector.' Orloff picked out three small plastic bags from the heap in front of him. 'Look at these. Gleanings from the mat in the kitchen, the rug in the hall, and the carpet in the living room. D'you see anything peculiar about them?'

Durieux stared. 'There's a bigger yield from the kitchen. That's normal, surely?'

'Is it? All three were cleaned the day before, very thoroughly. Marguerite Foucard walked wet sand into the house through the front door. You see the quantity yielded by the rug in the hall. Christine came in through the kitchen door. Look at the difference.' Orloff picked up a man's slipper. 'And Luc doesn't appear to have gone outside that morning.'

'Hey, wait!' The Inspector frowned. 'He was working on the repair to the wall. He must've changed his shoes in the kitchen.'

'Did he? Concrete dust was found on these slippers. But not a particle of sand, wet or dry.'

'That doesn't make sense, Commissaire.'

'Not yet. I'm not satisfied about the condition of the latch on the kitchen door,' said Orloff, suddenly changing direction.

'The girl's prints are on it, outside.'

'Agreed. But only hers. So why aren't Madame Basret's prints on that latch underneath Christine's? She would shut the door behind herself on leaving.'

'Luc let her out. His prints are on the key on the inside.' Durieux stopped, suddenly puzzled. 'That can't be right. He'd have to touch the inside of the latch, and there isn't a print on it. My God! The thing's been wiped. Inside and out.'

Orloff permitted himself a smile. 'I've enough to give our excellent *juge d'instruction* something to think about, and I want to see the girl again after I've spoken with him this afternoon. Have her brought here, please.'

Durieux decided not to waste breath on asking what other evidence was to be extracted from Christine Kergrist. 'Where do we start looking now?'

'With the obvious. The family. And La Foucard. Is there any word in from my office about that guy I saw her with at the hotel?'

With a conjuror's air of producing a rabbit from a hat, the Inspector laid a sheet of paper before the Commissaire. 'Came over the teleprinter just now.'

Orloff read out: ' "Jacques Hélory, antique dealer, query fence; sixty years of age; resident of Rennes." Now, that I find very interesting.'

'I've had de Montigny on the blower asking when his client can reclaim her things from the house.'

'I think we may oblige her,' said Orloff in a satisfied tone. 'Tell him we'll meet them at the house at four thirty. It's time I had a talk with Madame Foucard.'

Christine was surprised to find how much of a relief it was to be brought out of the prison, if only for a short while, to pass through streets where people were living ordinary lives, where time did not stand still. Even the unadorned offices of the *police judiciare* were a big improvement on the prison. The thought that she might be sent back to that place for a term of years seemed to stop her heart beating. Resolutely, she tried to banish the fear from her mind.

'You look brighter, Mademoiselle,' Commissaire Orloff greeted her in the barely furnished interrogation room.

The sight of him brought tears she was unwilling to shed pricking at her eyelids. 'I've something to hope for now,' she said simply.

'No promises,' he reminded her. 'I've yet more questions for you. First, tell me about Luc Plouviez. As dispassionately as you can, please. What sort of man was he?'

Christine gazed at an inward, beloved image. 'He was very good looking. Tall, well-set-up. Curly dark hair. Grey eyes.' She paused for a moment, then went on with a wry smile, 'I think he must have looked quite a dish in his naval uniform.'

'Not a typical Breton,' Orloff remarked.

'Foreign blood on his mother's side, Janine told me. Luc was a man of the world. He'd been all over the place. He had a broad outlook. He didn't think Tremerrec was the centre of the universe,' she added.

'And do you?' the Commissaire enquired.

'Not any more,' Christine said bleakly.

'Yet Luc came back here, presumably to settle.'

She shook her head. 'I don't think so. When I first met him, he was content to rest and recover from his wounds. Then he started to get his head together, start thinking about the future. I noticed a big change when I came back at the end of term. He wasn't going to let his disabilities hold him back from living a real life.'

'A brave man, then.'

'Oh, yes, Commissaire. Mentally as well as physically.'

'Did he discuss his plans with you?'

'Only in the most general of terms. But I'm sure he intended to be up and away once he was fit.'

'Taking you along with him?'

She blushed. 'I hoped so.'

'But you couldn't be sure?' Orloff persisted. 'After all, his family – '

She flared up: 'You've been listening to Maître Plouviez, which is more than Luc would have done. Anatole's an awful snob.'

'I understand he disapproves of your friendship with his son.'

'He disapproves of me, period. I'm not supposed to have any ambition, or even to use the brains I was born with. And I'm certainly not supposed to know any of the Plouviez socially. Sacha and I were at school together, that's all.'

'His father seems to think his son cares for you,' said Orloff, mildly. 'He termed it "puppy-love".'

Christine flushed. 'For once, we're in agreement. Poor Sacha. He doesn't find life easy.'

'What's wrong with him?'

'Parental tyranny. Sacha's supposed to follow in Anatole's footsteps. He's at law school and hates it. He wants to go to sea.'

'It's in the blood.'

'I guess that's what his father can't stand, being reminded of the family's origins.'

'There seems to be one in every generation who breaks free – Emile, Luc, and now Sacha,' Orloff remarked. 'Doesn't Maître Plouviez ever feel the call of the deep?'

'Only in the most gentlemanly fashion,' Christine replied with a grin. 'He has a yacht, what else? And he goes in for fancy fishing, for sport, though I imagine they eat the catch. When it's something eatable, that is. It's all part of his image.'

'How did Luc get on with him?'

'He kept him at a distance. But that applied to the whole family, except Sacha. Luc told me the women were all over him when he first came home. He couldn't bear it, and threw them out. There was an awful rumpus.'

'He lived alone, with just a daily housekeeper?'

'Janine was so good to him. She missed her husband terribly, though she put a good face on it. Looking after Luc filled a big gap, but she was very tactful. She didn't try to mother him. She knew independence was important to him. And she always took Sundays and public holidays off, but she'd leave his meals ready to be put in the oven.'

'Was she hostile to you, Mademoiselle?'

'I don't know,' Christine replied, honestly. 'I didn't think so, but she's very reserved.'

'What did you do when you were at the house, apart from giving a little medical help in changing dressings?'

'That didn't last long, Commissaire. The wounds were healed by the middle of July. Luc assumed that meant he was completely cured, although he still had a lot of pain. But that came from internal injuries which were never going to heal properly. Being blown up does terrible things to a human body.'

'Was that when he began repairing the garden wall?'

Christine's eyes sparkled with remembered indignation. 'He started on that when my mother dragged me off on a family visit for a couple of days. Poor Maman, she was trying to get me away from Luc. We did nothing but quarrel about him. The trip was a disaster. When I got back, Luc showed me his handiwork. I was horrified. I told him it was much too soon for so much exertion. He could've put himself back in hospital.'

'Did he take any notice?'

'Amazingly, yes. He didn't do any more at it. I imagine he

found it hard going, but was too proud to stop until I put my foot down.'

'Madame Basret says you were good for him.'

A lovely colour rose into her face, and Orloff had a glimpse of the girl as she was before tragedy overtook her. A prize for any man. He wondered how Sacha Plouviez had coped with losing her to his older cousin.

'What else did Luc do with himself?' he asked.

'He was working through Uncle Emile Plouviez's papers. I typed up his notes most days. Have you been in that room in the tower? It's stacked to the roof.'

'I've had a look inside a few of the boxes. What was Luc intending to do with those papers? The ones I saw were chiefly receipts. Emile Plouviez must have been an unusual sort of sailor. They're not commonly keepers of files.'

'That's what fascinated Luc. He was fond of Uncle Emile – he'd learned from him how to sail a boat – but until he dug into those boxes he'd no idea what an interesting life the old man had led. He thought it should be recorded, perhaps make a book out of it.'

'I'm told Uncle Emile made his fortune out East.'

'He certainly did. Luc told me he'd been there for the best part of forty years. He ran away to sea when he was nineteen, and no one saw or even heard of him again until he turned up in Tremerrec thirty years ago, rich and mysterious, accompanied by a Korean manservant named Lim, would you believe?'

'I am fascinated, Mademoiselle. Go on.'

'D'you really want to hear all this?' she said hesitantly. 'I can't imagine why Uncle Emile came back here. Luc says he quarrelled with all the family, and only took to him because he came across him mooning over the boat he had tied up at the back of the house. No one else was let over the doorstep.'

'Perhaps that was for security. That collection of furniture and *objets d'art* is very valuable.'

'It's a Plouviez obsession,' Christine agreed. 'Anatole festooned the house with barbed wire with a maximum security gate in it. And it was empty. There wasn't anything left to steal.'

Orloff caught her inflection. 'You went in. When?'

'Years ago. We'd be thirteen, I think. Sacha knew where the keys were kept and borrowed them. I think both of us wished he hadn't. It was quite horrid, empty and echoing and dark with all the windows boarded up.'

'And how did you like the house once it was furnished and lived in?'

Christine bit her lip. 'Not all that much better. The place has an atmosphere. I suppose I was remembering first impressions. Somebody wanted to buy it, but Luc wouldn't sell.'

'D'you know who?'

She shook her head. 'Whoever it was had approached Anatole. No name was mentioned. It must've been for the position, they can't have been inside. Luc was almost as bad as Uncle Emile for keeping people out, especially the family. I'm afraid I made matters worse.'

'Deliberately?'

'Just by being there,' said Christine ruefully. 'Madame Tremel, Anatole's sister, took it upon herself to announce the Plouviez clan's condemnation of the pair of us. I wouldn't care to repeat some of the words she used. It made a great July 14th celebration.'

A grim smile appeared on the Commissaire's face. 'Storming the Bastille of Devil's Bay, no less. Very diverting. What did Luc have to say?'

'Quite a lot, before he showed her the door. You wouldn't believe what old quarrels surfaced. I guess every family has a few skeletons in the cupboard. They surely rattled that day.' She looked down, as if unable to meet his eyes. 'Luc said afterwards it wasn't fair that I should have to put up with that sort of thing. I think that woman put the idea into his head that he should send me away, and he used the excuse of the other one coming back into his life to do it.'

'D'you suppose the family applauded the choice of Marguerite Foucard in your stead?'

Christine was surprised into a giggle. 'She looks as if she could eat the whole family for breakfast.'

'A redoubtable woman,' Orloff agreed. 'If it's any consolation to you, the housekeeper puts a different interpretation on the facts. She's convinced that Madame Foucard forced Luc into jilting you. Did he ever mention her, before the letter he sent you announcing their engagement?'

'No. But then, he rarely talked about himself, and never

81

about his naval service or where he'd been and what he'd done. I knew there must have been' – she gulped – 'other women.'

'You didn't ask?'

She shook her head. 'Never. I knew he'd tell me what he wanted me to know, in his own good time.'

The Commissaire's tufty eyebrows rose. 'You're a remarkable young woman. No curiosity?'

A shy, uncertain smile appeared. 'Yes, of course, I longed to know all about him. But Luc was a private sort of man. I suppose he'd learnt to keep secrets in the Navy.'

'Very likely,' Orloff agreed, having his own opinion of what sort of work Luc Plouviez had been doing. 'I can understand why Luc had no car. Did he have a boat?'

'No. Sacha took him out in his.'

'What sort of boat?'

'They all look much the same to me,' said Christine frankly. 'It's a little one, with an outboard motor. He used to tie it up at the back of the house.'

'Which house? His parents' or Luc's?'

'I was thinking of Luc's, but there could be a landing-stage at Sacha's home. They live upriver from Tremerrec.'

'Were these outings with Luc a regular feature?'

'All the summer, till I came home.' Colour rushed up into her face. 'I spoilt it all, for both of them. Sacha and I had a dreadful row over Luc.'

'When?'

'The middle of July. After Madame Tremel started stirring up the family. Sacha came over to Devil's Bay demanding to be told the truth.'

'What did you tell him?'

Her chin came up defiantly. 'I'd nothing to hide. I told him I loved Luc.'

'And what did Luc have to say?'

'He didn't see Sacha. He was up in the tower. Anyway, Sacha didn't go into the house. We yelled at each other on the rocks. Sacha – ' for a moment, her eyes blazed – 'Sacha seemed to think he had some rights over me.'

'And had he?'

'No, he did not! We were *copains*, friends, nothing more.'

'You must have known he cared for you, Mademoiselle. I refuse to believe you are devoid of feminine instinct.'

She sighed. 'I know I should have told him, but I didn't think he'd understand.'

'As, in effect, he didn't. You're an intelligent young woman. Hasn't it crossed your mind that Sacha might have killed Luc Plouviez?'

Christine's hands clenched into tight fists, so that the knuckles showed white. Hastily she hid them beneath the table.

'No,' she panted. 'Not Sacha.'

'The idea upsets you, Mademoiselle. Until this moment you have been so cool, perhaps a little too much. No sign of panic even with your whole future at risk. I wonder why.'

She did not answer.

Orloff waited, then continued, 'This isn't the moment to start holding out on me. You know perfectly well that Luc's family are prime suspects. A matter of inheritance.'

'Oh, but Luc left it all to charity.'

'Not quite. The contents of the house go to his relations. Unless I'm much mistaken, they're worth a fortune.'

Christine gulped. 'Oh, I see. I didn't think.'

'Quite,' said the Commissaire in a hard voice. 'I thought it was strange that you had not named the Plouviez family as possible suspects. You're trying to protect Sacha. Believe me, it won't help him – or you. It doesn't pay to play games with me, Mademoiselle.'

Chapter 7

Marguerite Foucard was so keen to collect her belongings from Luc Plouviez's house that she dragged her reluctant lawyer out to Devil's Bay well in advance of the hour of their appointment. They sat in her car at the end of the causeway, waiting, one resigned, the other drumming her fingers on the driving wheel.

The small sound eroded Bernard de Montigny's patience. 'I'm going to stretch my legs,' he announced, getting out.

He strolled to the path leading to The Chasm and began the steep climb. At the top, he peered down into the cleft, decided it was an ideal place for a murder, then stepped back hurriedly in irrational primeval alarm as he heard a footstep behind him.

Swinging round, he saw his client scrambling up in her high-heeled shoes and smart, tight frock.

'Orloff's got no business to keep us waiting,' she panted.

'We're in no position to complain, Madame.' He glanced at his watch. 'In any case, we're early.'

She was in no mood to respond to reason. 'He's doing it deliberately. To spite me.'

'You have a persecution mania, Madame,' he said shortly. 'I've seen no evidence that the Commissaire is doing anything but his job.'

'Who put him on to this case, anyway?' she demanded. 'Don't tell me our precious Minister of the Interior is really concerned about that little slut. Someone's pulling a stunt.'

Privately, Bernard agreed with her. Aloud, he said soothingly, 'There's no need to trouble yourself, Madame. Give your evidence concisely and truthfully and that will be all there is to it. It's a grave error to let a policeman of Orloff's calibre get the idea that you're holding something back.'

Marguerite let out a snort. 'He's using this as an excuse for prying.'

'Then perhaps you'd better tell me what there is to pry into.'

She turned away, her attention diverted, as a police car swept on to the beach.

'What a lot of *flics* for one paltry suitcase,' Marguerite remarked, as the Commissaire, Inspector Durieux and two gendarmes emerged from the car. Distastefully, she picked her way down the rocky path. 'I'll be glad to see the back of this place.'

'Last week you were talking about buying the house,' Bernard reminded her, in a spirit of malice.

She brushed it aside. 'A moment of sentimental weakness, Monsieur. I've got over it.'

He thought, 'And the loss of your fiancé, too.'

Orloff greeted them with suspicious urbanity which impressed neither, but for different reasons. Bernard was sure his client's persistent rudeness to the powerful man was more than unwise, and born out of a bad conscience. He waited for some blow to fall upon her.

Marguerite led them upstairs to the bedroom she had occupied. Inspector Durieux cleared the wardrobe of the few garments hanging there, handing each one to its owner only after searching the pockets, then started on the chest of drawers.

The Commissaire, missing nothing, stood to one side. 'When did you arrive here, Madame?'

'August 4th.'

'By invitation?'

She hesitated. 'We'd arranged it a long time ago.'

Bernard clenched his teeth at what was, at best, only a half-truth. The woman was a fool. Spite could land her in deep trouble.

'So, in effect, you surprised Monsieur Plouviez?' said Orloff, interpreting the lie.

Marguerite shrugged one shoulder and went on packing her clothes.

'How long did you stay?' he continued.

'A week. Then I went home for a few days. I told him I'd be back on the 15th. The Basret hag will confirm that, if you don't believe me,' she added belligerently.

'Quite,' said Orloff. 'Have you packed everything, Madame?'

He watched her close the suitcase, then went on, 'I have satisfied you in this matter, perhaps now you will do the same for me. What is your connection with Jacques Hélory?'

Marguerite stared at him, taken aback. 'Business,' she snapped.

'I'm aware of Monsieur Hélory's trade. He's an antique dealer. Is that your latest venture?'

She glanced sharply at her lawyer for guidance.

'It sounds a reasonable question, Madame,' Bernard replied, smooth tones covering annoyance at being left in the dark so that Orloff could jump something on him. 'It doesn't appear to be against your interest to answer. As far as I know,' he added, with utmost caution.

He was rewarded with a glare, but she accepted the advice. 'I'm not a dealer, Commissaire. On occasions, I've acted for friends who wished to dispose of things.'

'As a commission agent?'

The term left a disagreeable taste in her mouth, but she swallowed it. 'If you like.'

'And on behalf of whom are you acting at the moment? Or should I say, were? This house is full of highly negotiable objects.'

'I haven't done any business here in Brittany.'

'Yet Hélory was in Tremerrec last night. I saw you together.'

'The business we were discussing had nothing to do with Luc Plouviez,' she declared.

'Monsieur Hélory is a resident of Rennes. A fair drive from here, but not more than three hours, perhaps less. Your own alibi for the murder of Luc Plouviez is established, but I don't rule out the possibility of the existence of an accomplice, someone within – how shall I put it? – striking distance.'

Marguerite Foucard's face was suffused with dark colour, and her eyes bulged. 'I don't believe this,' she gasped.

'Had Hélory visited this house?'

'What if he had?'

'Please answer the question, Madame. When did he come here?'

She gazed daggers at him for a moment, then shifted her eyes to Bernard de Montigny's face and, finding no comfort there, back again to Orloff. 'August 6th or 7th,' she muttered.

'For what purpose? As a valuer?'

She sighed deeply. 'Luc wasn't about to sell off Uncle Emile's treasures. He wasn't short of cash. Jacques's visit was to me.'

The Commissaire was not impressed. 'You had your car here. You could have met him anywhere. What was so special about Hélory's visit that Luc Plouviez, a virtual recluse, would admit him to this house? Was it so that Hélory would be admitted again? On August 15th, for instance? Perhaps this wasn't a crime of passion after all, but some sort of highly-selective robbery of items for which unscrupulous collectors would pay high prices.'

The suggestion had a curious effect on Marguerite. Her colour returned to normal, and whatever danger she had felt threatened her, appeared to have retreated. A sour smile appeared on her full lips.

'Who're you trying to fool?' she jeered. 'I know what it is, that little tart's been flapping her eyelashes at you and you're looking for a scapegoat. You won't get her off by hanging it on to Jacques and me. There can't have been a robbery here, not without Janine Basret noticing. That woman went on as if she owned the place. She knows where everything is, down to the last spoon. Anything else you want to know?' she added, cheekily.

The Commissaire ignored the provocation. 'Not for the moment, Madame.'

Bernard jumped in. 'Is my client free to leave?' he asked, anxious to get her off the premises before she could cause more trouble.

'Certainly.'

'And go home, too?' Bernard pressed him.

'If she wishes. But I must ask her to remain available for questioning at any time.'

Marguerite opened her mouth to object, but Bernard quelled her with a frown. 'Madame Foucard will undertake to do that, Commissaire.'

'Stop poncing about as if I weren't in the same room,' she burst out. 'How long's this going to take?'

'At the moment, it's impossible to say,' Orloff replied. 'Not long. A few days only.'

'Very well, I'll give myself a vacation. I'll stay on in Tremerrec.' She turned on Bernard. 'And so will you, Maître, if you know what's good for you.'

He sighed, aware of a valuable client represented by this

tiresome woman. 'I'm at your service, Madame,' he said, and held open the door for her.

She swept out, leaving him to carry her suitcase. Flushing, and feeling a fool under the amused eyes of Orloff and Durieux, Bernard picked it up and followed her.

For such a stately figure, Marguerite could move with remarkable speed. There was no sign of her on the staircase. Descending, he found her standing beside the table in the centre of the hall exuding a strong impression of one kept waiting. With a martyr's sigh, she picked up her outsize handbag and accompanied him to the door.

Bernard bit back the acid words he longed to address to her. Not for the first time, he wished himself anywhere but in Brittany. 'You didn't tell me about Hélory,' he complained mildly.

'None of your business,' Marguerite shot back. 'Or Orloff's, either.'

Returning to Devil's Bay came as a nasty surprise to Christine. She had thought she was being taken back to the prison, which was a dreary enough prospect, but when the car turned for the coast, her heart sank. She had hoped never to see the place again.

It was a slight relief to see the beach deserted for the sacred hour of the evening meal, and no curious eyes to feast on her misfortune. Memories of that last terrible morning flooded over her, and started her trembling. She set her teeth and resolved not to break down.

The car halted at the foot of the climb to The Chasm, near where she had left her borrowed bicycle. Orloff appeared on the track leading to the house, and she was told to get out of the car. She waited apprehensively.

'I want you to help me with a reconstruction of your movements, Mademoiselle,' he said, with a sharp glance at her white face. 'It won't take long. Believe me, it's necessary. Now, think back. You've just arrived and parked your bike against a rock. What next?'

'I climbed up.'

'Right, we'll do that. Off you go.' He followed her up, halting her at the top. 'Can you remember where you stood to look down into The Chasm?'

Christine was vague, repelled by the idea of going over it all again. 'Somewhere here. Does it matter?'

He smiled. 'I've a fad for details.' He stepped forward and took up a position at the edge of the cleft. 'This is the first place to give one a good view down. I'm going to walk along the edge. Stop me when you think I've reached the spot where you stood.'

It was about halfway along the bare rock. Christine was bidden to join him.

'This is where I lost my nerve,' she said. 'I all but turned back. But I'm glad I didn't.'

'Unusual,' Orloff commented. 'Why? Had you gone away at that point you would have been under suspicion, but certainly not charged with murder.'

'I was with Luc when he died. When I first saw him, I thought he was dead, but I called his name and somehow he came back enough to know I was there. He held my hand for the last few moments. It means a great deal to me that he didn't die all alone.'

The Commissaire's eyebrows rose. 'Interesting, Mademoiselle. But hardly relevant.'

'Why not?' she flung back at him. 'What do I have to do to persuade you I'm innocent?'

'Persuasion doesn't come into it. I shall make my judgment solely on the evidence. So far, there is very little in your favour. Are you willing to help me look for fresh evidence – no matter who is implicated?'

Christine flushed. 'If you mean Sacha, I'm not afraid for him.'

'Then walk with me along this cliff,' Orloff invited, 'to check visibility. Inspector Durieux is down below. He'll shout the moment we come into view.'

They covered the length of the rock without a sound from below. Nor could they see the back of the house, where, in days gone by, Emile Plouviez had kept his boat. The view was blocked by a tumble of huge boulders, once a cliff, weathered smooth and shattered by storm and tide.

'Where did you climb down?' Orloff asked.

Christine pointed. 'Over there. It's not exactly a path but it's quite easy walking. I'd often gone that way.'

She led him down a gully to cut across the rocks to meet the track to the house. Orloff shouted and Durieux came round to join them at the front door.

'We didn't get a glimpse of you, Commissaire,' he announced.

'We didn't see you, either. That settles one point: if there was a boat tied up round there, Christine couldn't see it. Nor would anyone in it know she was there.' He turned to the girl. 'We've arrived at the house. What did you do? In minute detail, please.'

'I went in through the kitchen door.'

Orloff wagged a long finger at her. 'That won't do. You're jumping ahead. The track brings you out at the front of the house. Why didn't you use that door?'

'It was locked.'

'How d'you know?'

'I tried it. Oh, I see what you mean about detail.'

She won approval. 'Good girl. Go on.'

She frowned, reliving the moment. 'Luc usually left that door open, so I thought the place must be empty and I felt such a fool, working myself up to face the pair of them, only to find no one here. It didn't seem right. I was sure they had to be somewhere about. I banged the knocker, several times – ' she broke off, biting her lip.

'Yes?' Orloff prompted her. 'You've remembered something. What?'

For a moment Christine did not reply, then she said slowly, 'I was wondering why I bothered going round to the kitchen door. It was a holiday: Janine wouldn't be there, and no one had come when I knocked.'

'Hasn't anyone asked you?'

'Yes, they must have done.' She seemed confused and glanced at Durieux. 'You did.'

'That's right. You said you couldn't get a reply at the front so you went round to the back. I didn't probe. It seemed a good enough answer to me. What's wrong with it?' The Inspector glanced at Orloff. 'I've missed something,' he added crossly.

'Hardly your fault, since the witness has begun only now to think clearly about what happened that morning. Are you making any progress, Mademoiselle?'

'I don't know. The place didn't feel right,' she said, hesitantly.

'There was something. A movement, or a sound even. I – I had the impression there was someone inside.'

Inspector Durieux let out a hiss of exasperation, instantly suppressed.

Christine turned on him. 'What difference would it have made if I'd remembered this at the time? It wouldn't have made you believe me. Does it impress you, Commissaire?' she added recklessly.

'That's a question you don't ask,' Orloff snapped. 'Let's get on with this.' He led them round the house to the kitchen door. 'You found this door unlocked?'

'Open, Commissaire, standing ajar.'

He stepped inside, the others following. 'Please remove your shoes, Mademoiselle.'

Christine stared. Then, with a bewildered shake of her head, she kicked off her sandals. Inspector Durieux picked them up and dropped them into a plastic bag. With a nod to the Commissaire, he went back outside.

'We have another pair for you,' Orloff assured the girl. 'We don't expect you to go barefoot.'

'What d'you want with my shoes?'

'Sand, Mademoiselle. It's not been very hot today. There was rain this morning and we've added a little to that to create as nearly as possible the condition of the sand when you arrived here on the morning of the murder.'

'You want to see how much I picked up? How will that help?'

'Wait and see,' said the Commissaire. 'Now, a further ordeal. Madame Basret is coming to check over the contents of the house, in case anything is missing. Will you help her?'

'All you need is the inventory, Luc said everything was checked off as it was unpacked. You know his mother had everything put into store?'

'How very efficient and convenient for poor policemen,' said Orloff. 'Where is this inventory?'

'In Luc's desk. Bottom drawer, left hand side.' She ran out into the hall, then stopped abruptly. 'I'm sorry, Commissaire, I can't fetch it for you. That room – ' She put a hand to her mouth.

The Commissaire nodded and went past her into the living room to fetch it himself.

On the other side of the front door voices were raised in

argument, one of them a woman's. At once, the Commissaire reappeared, carrying a sheaf of much-thumbed pages. Then the front door opened and Inspector Durieux came in, shutting it behind him.

'I don't know how they got past my man,' he said, annoyed. 'Maître Plouviez and his sister are outside. Someone,' he added, in tones that boded ill for the unfortunate responsible, 'told them you were here.'

'Don't let it bother you,' Orloff replied calmly. 'It suits me well enough to speak to them now. I know what they want.'

'Possession of this place, Commissaire.'

'Plouviez is the executor of Luc's will. I imagine he wants to get on with the job. He'll have to be patient for a little longer. When's the valuer coming to see the contents?'

'Tomorrow morning. Will you want to go round with him?'

Orloff shook his head. 'One of your best men can be my eyes and ears. What I want is an estimate of the total value. I think it will surprise you. By the way, I hope this fellow isn't one of Plouviez's friends.'

Durieux grinned. 'I doubt it. He's coming from Nantes.'

'That should be far enough away. I'll see these people in the kitchen. I don't want them tramping round the rest of the house. Has Madame Basret arrived?'

'She's in the kitchen, Commissaire.'

'Get her out before you let in our uninvited guests. I don't want them to see her or Mademoiselle Christine.' He glanced at the girl. 'I must ask you to wait in one of the cars. Our tour of the house will have to wait until these others have gone.'

'I'm in no hurry,' said Christine bitterly.

She encountered an enigmatic stare, then Orloff strode off to the kitchen to receive Anatole Plouviez and his sister.

There was a strong family likeness. Simone Tremel had a masculine, no-nonsense air about her. No one could pretend she was a beauty, or ever had been, but this was a formidable woman. She was dressed in expensive but plain clothes, and sat with a handbag large enough to class as an offensive weapon balanced upon spread knees. Brother and sister sat on hard chairs on the other side of the well-scrubbed table and stared grimly at the Commissaire.

'You wished to see me?' he said, with no hint of welcome in his voice.

Anatole took a deep breath. 'We – Luc's family, that is – are concerned about the present situation with regard to the estate. There's a lot of work to be done, papers in this house which must be dealt with, arrangements to be made.' He paused but received no encouragement. 'I'm sure you appreciate . . . such an unfortunate business . . . If you could give us some idea . . .' He tailed off uncertainly under Orloff's cool stare.

His sister cut in: 'When do we get the keys to this house?'

Anatole's discomfort increased. 'Simone, please!' he frowned.

Madame Tremel had lost all patience with him. 'You won't get anywhere by treading all round the point. I don't know why this case has been reopened when it's as plain as the nose on your face that the murderer has been caught. There can be no earthly reason why the police should keep us out of here and prevent you from getting on with settling the estate.'

'I regret, Madame, that Maître Plouviez will have to wait until I've completed my enquiries,' the Commissaire told her in arctic tones. 'As he is well aware. But now that you're here, I have some questions of my own to put to you.'

Ugly colour rose into her face. Her brother cast her a look which said plainly: now see what you've started!

'Certainly, Commissaire,' he said, anxious to regain lost ground. 'I promise you our full cooperation. I hope you'll pardon our intrusion on your valuable time. My sister is a little overwrought. A murder in our family is an outrage.'

Simone Tremel had no time for her brother's diplomacy. 'It comes of encouraging a girl out of the gutter,' she exploded. 'I told Luc he was a fool. But did he listen? When did that man ever take notice of anyone?'

'You knew him when he was young, of course,' said Orloff. 'Both of you.'

'Indeed we did.' Anatole rushed in before his sister had time to open her mouth. 'There were four of us cousins: Simone and myself; Paul and Luc. We all lived in Tremerrec. Luc was younger than the rest of us by a good ten years. Paul was the eldest, then my sister, then me, and lastly, Luc. Paul was my best friend. It was a great blow to me when he drowned,' he added soberly.

'It was your salvation, more like!' Simone chipped in witheringly. 'Paul was a layabout, and you'd have gone to the bad with him if he'd lived.'

Orloff hid a smile. There was profit in enraging this woman. 'You preferred Luc, Madame?'

'Him?' she snorted. 'We never took any account of Luc. He was a loner, always off by himself. We found out why, of course, when Uncle Emile's Will was read. Luc had spent his time sucking up to him. He inherited the lot.'

Anatole said firmly, 'The Commissaire doesn't want to hear about old quarrels, it's all water under the bridge.'

Simone snorted. 'Luc never cared a button for any of us until he needed help. Then you were permitted to work your fingers to the bone getting this place fit for habitation for him to come home to. You and Yvonne,' she added, extending her resentment to her sister-in-law.

'Be reasonable,' Anatole snapped back. 'He was in no condition to unpack all that stuff himself.'

'And what reward did you receive? The brush-off, as soon as he was installed, and now he's gone, just a share in the furniture, while everything else goes to charity.'

'That Will was made twenty years ago,' he replied, losing all patience. 'I'm sure he'd have changed it, but the poor fellow didn't get the chance.'

Orloff, enjoying the glimpse of family jealousy, decided to take a hand. 'Once he was married, the situation would have changed,' he suggested.

Brother and sister broke off their quarrel to gaze at him, united by a sudden common apprehension.

Anatole was the first to recover. 'I was expecting him to call me. It's hardly relevant now.'

'When did you last see him?'

'Sometime in May.'

'I was here in July,' said Madame Tremel, still belligerent. 'Word had reached me about that little trollop. I gave Luc a piece of my mind. And her.'

'How was that received?'

Her lips tightened. 'I prefer not to say, now Luc's dead. But he took notice. He sent her away.'

'In favour of an older woman.'

'A much more suitable match,' Anatole put in smoothly. 'Luc needed someone to look after him. Madame Foucard's a fine person. And rich,' he added reverently.

'Was that likely to influence Luc Plouviez?'

'Hardly,' Simone snapped. 'Uncle Emile left him a fortune.'

'It's not quite as large as popular conjecture had it,' Anatole corrected her. 'But he had no financial worries. The capital sum had appreciated over the years that Luc was in the Navy. I flatter myself that it was well invested. He never drew on it, living on his pay. He'd advanced in his career, making captain's rank.'

'So the charity is going to do rather well,' said Orloff pleasantly, and received no answering smiles. 'However, the contents of this house will fetch an acceptable sum. How many people share?'

Simone Tremel's mouth dropped open, then shut again with a snap.

Anatole looked shocked. 'Surely, you don't – ?' He could not bring himself to finish.

'It's my job,' said Orloff grimly. 'Heirs are bound to come under scrutiny. Who are they?'

'Quite a lot of people. Everyone in the family gets something. Goods, of course, not cash,' Anatole replied.

Orloff foresaw a great deal of legwork ahead. 'So, for instance, where was your immediate family on the day of Luc Plouviez's murder?'

'We were all together,' Madame Tremel announced with an air of triumph. 'We always come over for August 15th, my husband and our children, and two of the old aunts. We've done it every year since I was married.'

'Was Luc invited?'

'He couldn't have come. He was expecting Madame Foucard,' said Anatole hurriedly. 'We can't include everyone.'

'Where was this party held?'

'On my yacht. We sailed down the river and had a barbecue on one of the islands.'

At the mention of the alfresco meal Simone's lips tightened, as if in an unpleasant reminder, but when the Commissaire looked to her for confirmation, she merely nodded.

'The young people like these things,' Anatole muttered.

'You were all together from what time?' Orloff enquired.

'We drove over quite early,' Simone told him. 'We arrived in time to go to Mass in the Cathedral.'

'Ten thirty,' Anatole supplied. 'It was after twelve before we sailed, which was later than we had intended, but at least we missed the storm.'

Once again, Madame Tremel screwed up her mouth. This time, her brother ignored her. 'We will all make statements,' he said firmly, giving her an admonitory glance.

'Inspector Durieux will arrange that tomorrow,' Orloff informed him. Rising, he pushed back his chair to indicate the end of the interview. 'On the matter of the keys to this house, Monsieur, I shall keep them for no longer than I deem necessary.'

Madame Tremel looked daggers at him but, at a warning glance from her brother, followed in silence as Orloff led them through into the hall and to the front door.

The Commissaire returned to the kitchen as the Inspector ushered Janine Basret and Christine through the back door, to commence the check of Luc's portable valuables. It was achieved remarkably quickly. Marguerite Foucard had been right: the housekeeper knew where everything should be, and Christine confirmed that nothing seemed to be missing. It was not until they came downstairs into the entrance hall that there was a break.

Orloff stared down at the table in the middle. 'The bowl's not here. The little one holding loose change. It was here yesterday.'

There was a moment's tense silence.

'I haven't been in here since the murder,' Janine muttered defensively. 'Anyone could've taken it. There was never more than a few francs, no great loss.'

Durieux said furiously, 'Are you accusing the police, Madame?' He glanced at Orloff. 'I'll take those guards apart. I won't have souvenir-hunting.'

The Commissaire was thinking along other lines. Anatole Plouviez had walked with him to the front door, not missing a chance to talk. But his sister had lagged behind . . . and on her arm was a capacious handbag.

Chapter 8

Commissaire Orloff was far from satisfied. 'There are too many loose ends,' he complained.

'A couple of days ago, I didn't know there were any,' Durieux replied ruefully. 'I'd like to think Christine is innocent.'

'Then let's try to find out. Imagine that she is not the killer. What other possibilities are there? Who has a motive?'

'Try the Plouviez family, standing to gain a good deal of valuable assets from the distribution of the contents of the house. I shouldn't have overlooked that. I didn't know this stuff was valuable. And they all alibi each other.'

'You smell a conspiracy? It was given to us in only the most general terms. That must be examined. There might be some holes. And there is one particular member of the family who has a personal motive: Sacha, the rejected lover. He might have managed to slip away from the party. Nor must we overlook Madame Foucard. I may be blinded by a certain prejudice, but I refuse to accept that her presence in this affair is purely coincidental.'

'She can't have been the killer herself,' the Inspector reminded him.

'Agreed, though I have my doubts about her statement. To arrive here at the time she did, she'd have had to leave Paris in the middle of the night. My guess is that she stayed overnight somewhere, but doesn't wish us to know about it.'

Durieux grinned. 'Rennes, for instance?'

'You read my mind,' said Orloff grimly. 'The *police judiciaire* there should have pulled in Jacques Hélory by now, or perhaps he has turned up again in Tremerrec. He's the obvious accomplice.'

'An antique dealer, too. But the motive couldn't have been robbery, Commissaire. The only thing that's missing is the bowl in which Luc used to keep loose change. And that's only gone today.'

'That doesn't mean a robbery wasn't intended. Suppose Christine all but surprised our operator in the act. He – or she – had to make a dash for freedom through the back door.'

'Out to a boat?'

'Possibly. Or on foot to a car parked some distance away, down the lane leading to the farm.'

'Where does that leave Christine Kergrist?'

'Still in custody,' Orloff replied coolly. 'What I am saying now is pure supposition. It is based on the fact that there seems to be a surplus of sand in the kitchen. It will be interesting to know exactly how much we get off her shoes this evening. If I'm correct in this, we will be able to establish the presence of a third person in this house on the day of the murder. What that means, at this stage, is anyone's guess, but it is enough for me to report to the *juge d'instruction* that the matter requires further investigation. I have an appointment with him in the morning.'

Inspector Durieux probed no further. Only a fool could not perceive the object of the Commissaire's attack: he was out to nail Marguerite Foucard for something, and not necessarily the murder of Luc Plouviez.

'You may send Christine back to the prison, now,' Orloff said serenely. 'Where's Madame Basret?'

'Waiting in the kitchen.'

The Commissaire nodded and took himself off. He found Janine sitting at the table, utterly dejected. She looked up, gazing at him out of dull eyes. He took a seat on the other side of the scrubbed board.

'Was it so hard, Madame, coming back in here?'

She nodded, tears springing to her eyes. 'She looks so pale and thin, poor lass, but when you think what she's done . . .'

'Do *you* think so, Madame? You know Christine better than I do. What's your opinion?'

Janine shot him a glance of pure terror. 'She was so sensible. She's not a silly girl, and she's not hot tempered, either.' She rubbed a workworn hand over her face. 'I went along with what I was told, but now I've seen her again . . . God, what a mess it is.'

Orloff fixed an inexorable eye on her. 'Madame, I see you're

98

distressed. Whatever it is that you fear, I assure you it would be better if you confided in me.'

She shook her head. 'I can't be bothering you with my foolish fancies.'

'If Christine is innocent, someone else has to be guilty. You may be shielding someone without realising it.' He paused invitingly, but Janine did not respond. 'How long had you known Luc Plouviez?'

The question took her by surprise. 'Since he was a boy, I suppose. Why?'

'I'm interested in him and his whole family. Did you know his Uncle Emile?'

'I was a young wife when he built this house,' Janine replied, evidently feeling herself on steadier ground. 'We gave him help when he needed it.'

'I imagine his arrival caused a stir?'

'It was the biggest event in years. Everyone had forgotten about him, though I'm told he used to get drunk in Port Briac every night before he went to sea. He'd lost that habit by the time he came back. Emile Plouviez lived like a recluse, Commissaire, with only Lim, his manservant, in the house.'

'The Plouviez family must have been surprised to see him. Were they pleased?' Orloff enquired.

Janine let out a sharp crack of laughter. 'That lot? Properly put their noses out of joint, did Emile. He'd come home to end his days, not to rejoin the family and put his hand in his pocket to settle debts. He soon choked them off. The youngsters found him exciting, of course.'

'They would be, who?' Orloff prompted her as she paused.

'Anatole and Paul, chiefly. Emile considered them impertinent, and told them to be off. The only one he liked was Luc, who was only a child. He'd be about ten when Emile came home. He wanted to go to sea, that's what appealed to Emile. And the fact that the rest of the family disapproved. But Emile put the screws on them, somehow, and they let him join the Navy. He was at sea when the boat sank, or he'd have been in it, too. His mother wouldn't let Luc come home for his brother's funeral,' she added, with the air of raking up an old scandal.

'Why not?'

'Berthe Plouviez gave out that Luc would be too upset, but the truth was that Paul was her favourite and she couldn't bear that he was taken and Luc left. She didn't want to see him. She cleared up all his affairs for him, closed the house, put everything in store and arranged with her brother-in-law, Anatole Plouviez, to look after it all. Then she hanged herself.'

'Didn't he come back for the funeral of the uncle who'd helped him and left him a fortune, too?'

Janine looked surprised. 'There couldn't be a funeral, could there? This is a cruel coast, bodies aren't always found. Emile was never recovered, or his man, only the wreckage of the boat, and Paul's drowned body, Emile's cap and Lim's scarf and one of his shoes.' She shivered. 'It's no wonder this house got a bad reputation. And now Luc's gone, too.'

'My job is to catch his murderer, Madame,' said Orloff. 'Give me what help you can. Tell me, did Luc receive any letters the week before he died?'

Her brow wrinkled. 'I can't recall that he did.'

'Did he have any visitors?'

'None,' she said firmly, 'unless they came after seven o'clock when I went home.'

'Did he ask for the taxi to take him out?'

'Yes. On Saturday morning.'

'Where did he go?'

'Only as far as the village,' Janine replied. 'I went with him to do a bit of shopping for extra groceries for Madame Foucard's visit.'

'What did Luc do?'

'He went to the post office.'

'For stamps? Mailing letters?'

She shook her head. 'I did that for him. I expect he wanted to use the phone.'

Orloff sat back, perceiving a chink of light in the obscurity of the investigation. 'I don't suppose he told you whom he phoned?'

'Monsieur Luc never discussed his affairs with me, Commissaire. He'd have told me if he'd invited someone to stay.' She caught her breath. 'Could he have been asking someone to visit on the 15th?'

'That's supposition, Madame, attractive though it may be. Let's see if we can make it a little more substantial. Apart from his own family and Christine and you, how many people did Luc Plouviez know in this district?'

Janine thought about it. 'Very few, I suppose. The bank manager, the doctor, one or two tradesmen . . .' she trailed off. 'That's not much help.'

'Tell me if you think of anyone else,' Orloff replied, undaunted. 'I've one more question for you, Madame. When Luc Plouviez was found he was wearing slippers. Did he wear them all the time? Did he go out in the garden in them, for instance?'

'Oh, no, Monsieur Luc was meticulous. He wore slippers in the house and changed into shoes to go out. You can't set foot outside this place without picking up sand and tramping it in. He knew I didn't like that on my clean floors.'

Inspector Durieux slipped in, discreetly stationing himself to one side of the Commissaire, ready to listen. But he was too late. Orloff closed his notebook and sent the witness home.

'That's quite enough for one day, Inspector. Go home to your wife and family.' He smiled. 'I'm aware that I demand long hours of my colleagues. Take comfort from the thought that I shall be gone all the sooner.'

Durieux grinned. 'Anything special for the morning, Commissaire?'

'Find me Jacques Hélory.'

Bernard de Montigny sat in the hotel bar, reading a newspaper and keeping an eye on the door. The moment the tall figure of Orloff crossed his vision, he pounced.

'A word with you, please, Commissaire.'

Orloff was at the reception desk, glancing through a note which the clerk had handed to him. He looked up. 'I'm hungry,' he said shortly. 'Join me, if you wish.'

It was not what Bernard would have chosen, but he had had a long wait and the fact was that, he, too, wanted his dinner. Yet he regretted the feeling of intimacy brought by a shared meal.

Orloff, whom he knew to have an uncanny knack of accurately sizing up his fellow men, put his finger on the sore spot. 'I hope your mother is well, Monsieur?' he enquired politely, with a merciless smile.

Bernard gritted his teeth. 'I believe so. We don't see very much of her,' he said, hoping he was imagining the snarl he detected behind his words. 'Her business keeps her in England.' Hastily he changed the subject. 'Maître Plouviez was here a short while ago. He asked me to convey his apologies.'

The Commissaire looked amused. 'I can imagine. Are you acquainted with his family?'

'No, thank God!'

'He's lent you a temporary office, hasn't he?'

'I don't propose to live in his pocket,' Bernard replied grimly. 'I'm occupying his waiting room purely for my own convenience. I don't fancy being tête-à-tête with Madame Foucard in a bedroom here.'

'I wouldn't recommend it,' Orloff agreed. 'I imagine you're anxious to return to Paris?'

'I've a heap of work waiting.'

'Then perhaps we may help each other. I don't accept her account of her relationship with the late Luc Plouviez.'

'She's convinced it's none of your business. I assume she means it has no bearing on the murder,' Bernard said cautiously.

'Since when was Marguerite Foucard a judge of that? Her reticence suggests she may be engaged in some illegal act.'

'Are you asking me to act as an informer?' Bernard demanded.

'Far from it,' Orloff replied urbanely. 'I wouldn't like to see you involved as an accomplice.'

'I'm not. Madame Foucard won't tell me a thing, either. She's got over whatever nerves she had. She's not frightened, Commissaire. On the contrary, she seems pleased with herself. To be honest, I don't know if it's innocence or devilish fine acting,' he added, in the spirit of building up defences in advance of possible catastrophe.

'That's a question I've been trying to answer for ten years,' Orloff told him. 'She's a careful operator. Now tell me why you were lying in wait for me. Not, surely, just to pass on your colleague's apologies?'

Bernard shook his head. 'I was thinking along the lines of how long am I to be kept hanging round here?'

'That depends on your client, Monsieur.'

'And she depends on you.'

'Then persuade her to open up, Maître. Where is she now?'

'I saw her go out some time ago.'

'Then it will have to wait until the morning. Can you bring

her to my office at half past ten? I've another call to make tonight.'

Jules Kergrist had waited up. 'I hope I haven't brought you out on a fool's errand, Commissaire,' he said anxiously, as he admitted a late visitor.

'The note you left at the hotel promised me something, Brigadier, but don't worry if it's a dead end. I'm used to those.'

'I'm afraid I'm clutching at straws,' he went on apologetically, as he brought his visitor into the parlour.

'And who's to blame you? What have you got?'

'The present whereabouts of a bad-hat by the name of Pierre Basret.'

Orloff had his notebook out. 'What relation to the housekeeper?'

'Youngest child. Thirty-two years of age. Unmarried. Criminal record as long as your arm.'

'For what?'

'Breaking and entering; robbery, occasionally with violence. He's just done a stretch. Been out a couple of months.'

'Where is he?'

'In Morlais, doing a job of sorts, casual labouring. He's not welcome at the Basret farm. His brother won't have him.'

'What about the mother?'

Kergrist shrugged. 'Some women make a point of not looking facts in the face. He's her favourite. My wife's sure Janine is dead scared that Pierre killed Luc Plouviez.'

'Offer me a motive,' Orloff invited.

'There was some trouble years ago, shortly after the house was closed up. Pierre'd be about thirteen and already heading for a life of crime. The lad was obsessed with a notion of buried treasure in that place.'

'I was told there'd never been a break-in. I found that difficult to swallow.'

'Pierre's escapade never became official police business, Commissaire. I was asked to give Pierre a talking-to, on a friendly basis. It was a waste of time, of course, but he didn't have another go at the house. He couldn't. His father and Anatole Plouviez between them had the place surrounded with rolls of barbed wire. It was all taken away when Luc came home.'

'So we have Pierre Basret out of prison and the house un-guarded. Would Luc have let him in?'

'Why not? He'd known him as a boy. Pierre would only have to say his mother had sent him.' Kergrist paused, then added, 'I don't know if Pierre Basret still wants to hunt for Emile Plouviez's treasure, if it exists, but I do know he's a damned sight more likely to be a killer than my daughter.'

Marie Kergrist slipped into the room, bearing a tray of coffee and cognac.

'How is Christine today, Commissaire?' she asked, handing him a cup, assuming he had seen the girl.

'Well enough. She appears to have stamina. I'm developing a considerable respect for that young lady, Madame. She's a clever girl.'

Marie's eyes shone. 'You're satisfied she's innocent? That's wonderful!'

'No, no, the Commissaire didn't say that,' Kergrist muttered in sudden anxiety.

Orloff smiled. 'You're going too fast for me, Madame. All I can say, so far, is that there are grounds for making a further investigation. I must warn you that Christine won't be released until another suspect is in custody.'

The Brigadier understood him all too well. 'Cases can drag on for years!' Marie looked ready to faint.

'Quite so. In the interests of all concerned, we need a quick result. Tell me, Madame – your home was near Devil's Bay – what were these tales of buried treasure?'

'I never paid much attention,' Marie confessed. 'They always sounded a bit daft to me. You should ask my father. There's precious little about the place that he doesn't know. His name's Henri Drouon and his farm's halfway between the bay and Port Briac, on the back road.'

'It doesn't much matter whether the treasure exists or not, only that Pierre Basret thinks it does,' Kergrist pointed out. 'Years ago, I tried to tell him the house had been stripped and there was nothing left in it, but he wouldn't have it. Thick as two planks, he is. He's never learned there's no such thing as easy money, nor likely to, now.'

'I'll pull him in,' Orloff promised and left after a polite interval.

Outside, the steep narrow street was ill lit, pools of darkness marking the irregular line of the old houses. He stepped out on to the cobbled road and the pale gleam of the street lights. Almost at once, he heard a step behind him. He turned swiftly, in time to see a figure dodge back into the shadows.

As if satisfied, he walked on a few paces, listening carefully until he was sure his follower was on the move again, then, at a turn in the road, stepped quietly into a darkened doorway and waited. A moment or two later, a form hugging the shelter of the houses all but crashed into him. Orloff reached out and clamped a large hand on an arm. There was a gasp and a futile attempt at escape.

'If you've mugging in mind, my friend, I don't advise it,' said the Commissaire, dragging his captive out into the light. 'Who are you?'

He had in his grip a young man of middle height, brown haired and faintly familiar.

'I'm not a mugger, Commissaire.' He stared up at his captor. 'If I were, I'd pick on someone my own size.'

Orloff did not relax his hold. 'So you know who I am. Your name?'

'Sacha Plouviez.'

'I should have known. There's a likeness to your father.'

'I don't call that a compliment,' Sacha replied, rubbing a released and bruised arm.

'Why were you following me? You were behind me when I left the hotel and I suppose you've been standing in the street waiting for me.'

'Could I talk to you?'

'What about?'

Sacha was surprised. 'Christine, of course. She didn't kill Luc.'

Orloff sighed. 'What am I to make of that? Are you offering me evidence or conjecture? If it's evidence, you're coming forward a bit late in the day, aren't you?'

The young man shook his head vigorously. 'When Christine was arrested, my father sent me to Rennes, on the excuse of helping my uncle – he's a lawyer, too – and I've been there ever since, until Aunt Simone decided to drive over today. Are you going to get Christine off?'

'My part, Monsieur, is to uncover the truth about Luc Plouviez's murder, whatever that may be,' Orloff told him in a hard voice. 'Do you have any fresh evidence?'

'Only that I know she couldn't commit such a crime,' Sacha replied, slightly dejected. 'I told Inspector Durieux several times. Father said I was making a nuisance of myself, but I had to do something.'

'You may walk back to the hotel with me and answer a few questions,' said the Commissaire, starting up the hill again. 'And I want straight answers. Did you quarrel with Luc over Christine?'

'I heard what my aunt was saying about her. I couldn't stand it. I went to see Luc, but Christine caught me. She bawled me out.'

'You were jealous?'

'I love her, Commissaire. I only wanted her to be happy,' said Sacha in a hurt tone. 'I had to know if he meant to marry her.'

'His intentions, in effect? How very old fashioned. What did you do when you heard that Luc had jilted Christine?'

'I tried to see her. She refused to talk to me. I can't blame her. None of my people wanted her in the family. Aunt Simone only said what they were thinking.'

'Did you tackle Luc?'

'I thought about it, but then I decided I was being a fool and I'd better leave it alone. If he didn't want her, she might come back to me – eventually,' he said miserably.

They turned into the town square. Orloff said abruptly, 'Where were you on August 15th?'

'There was a family party.'

'So I've heard. Tell me exactly what happened that morning.'

Sacha seemed to hang back, then sighed. 'It was pretty grim. There was the usual row with Father over breakfast.'

'What about?'

'My studies, and the mediocre results I had with the exams at the end of term. I'd had as much as I could take. I needed a bit of space.'

'You ducked the party?'

'Oh, no. I'd have had the lot of them on my back. I took off in my *autoche* – sorry,' he corrected himself at Orloff's sudden frown over the slang. 'My car, and left them to it for a couple of hours.'

106

'Where did you go?'

'Nowhere in particular. I just drove around, stopped and cooled off a bit, and got back to Tremerrec in time for the festivities. If you could call them that. Does it matter?'

'It might,' Orloff replied tartly. 'I know about the late start of your family party. Obviously they were waiting for you. It's crystal clear you're not cut out to be a lawyer. You've just destroyed the alibi your father attempted to give you.'

In the glare of a street lamp, the young man's face was white, and his mouth gaped with shock.

'Hadn't it occurred to you that you are as much a discarded lover as Christine Kergrist? So let's have it in detail. Where did you go that morning? And, more to the point, can you produce any witnesses?'

Sacha was stopped in his tracks. 'You're accusing *me* of Luc's murder?'

'You had a motive. See where championing Christine has got you,' Orloff said provocatively.

'I don't care. I didn't kill him any more than she did.'

'Be at my office at the PJ in Lannion tomorrow morning at eleven,' Orloff replied, and walked across to the hotel entrance.

Behind him, an angry voice exclaimed, 'Sacha! Where've you been? I've walked the streets for a couple of hours looking for you.'

'Father, won't you ever let go?' Sacha cried in an anguished voice. 'What the hell does it matter where I've been? I've my own life to live. At dinner you told me to get out of your sight. So I did.'

The Commissaire had turned to watch the comedy. Anatole Plouviez, very red in the face, suddenly became aware of his audience.

'Good heavens, Commissaire! I didn't see you.' He turned to his son. 'What – '

'I require his presence in my office tomorrow morning, Monsieur,' Orloff cut in. 'I should appreciate your attendance, too?'

'May I ask why?'

'Sacha will explain. Goodnight, Messieurs.' And Orloff stalked into the hotel.

A fresh spectacle met his eyes. A conference was in progress at the reception desk, with the clerk, the manager, Bernard de Montigny and a small man standing with his back to the door as the participants. Orloff's appearance broke it up, as the manager spotted him and dodged round the others in the hopes of reaching him first. He was hardly quick enough. Four people started talking at once.

Orloff towered over them. 'We'll go into your office, if you please, Monsieur,' he commanded, singling out the manager.

For a second the man stared at him, then, muttering compliance, made for a door behind the desk, the others filing after him.

The Commissaire shut the door. 'What's the matter?' he demanded. 'Monsieur de Montigny, you tell me,' he added, as four mouths opened.

'We don't know where Madame Foucard is,' Bernard said, simply.

'She was supposed to meet me at nine o'clock,' the small man declared.

Orloff gazed at him, feeling only faint satisfaction at a problem solved. 'Monsieur Jacques Hélory, I believe? I've been looking for you.'

The antique dealer stared back warily. 'I can't imagine why, Commissaire,' he replied, valiantly.

'That can wait. Why the panic over Madame Foucard? So far, only Monsieur Hélory is inconvenienced by her absence. How firm was this appointment?'

'She phoned me this afternoon – '

'Where were you, Monsieur?'

'Brest, if that matters. She insisted I came over this evening.'

'Madame Foucard booked a room for Monsieur Hélory, and a table in the restaurant for nine o'clock,' said the reception clerk, a pretty girl who did not care to be left out of things and was glad now of a chance to get in a word.

'What time was that?'

'Straight after her telephone call, Commissaire. It would be around six.'

'I saw her go out after that,' Bernard offered. 'Shortly after eight.'

'It's nearly midnight now.' The manager wished to assert himself. 'I've checked her room. Her things are there but her car is not in the car park.'

'Do you have its number?'

'Yes, Commissaire.' He snapped his fingers at the clerk, who scurried out to fetch the information.

'You know her better than anyone, Monsieur Hélory,' said Orloff. 'Has she friends in this district? Apart from her late fiancé's family, that is.'

Hélory shrugged. 'She isn't on visiting terms with them. Besides, we'd matters to discuss, and not much time to do it. Madame Foucard's a business-like woman. She would have left a note for me if anything had cropped up unexpectedly.'

Orloff studied his face, unattractive though it was, with a bad skin framed by greasy, slicked-back hair. 'I take the point, Monsieur. We must accept that Marguerite Foucard is missing.'

Chapter 9

There was still no sign of her the following morning, when, with the utmost reluctance, Jacques Hélory presented himself at Orloff's temporary office. He was accompanied by Bernard.

'In the absence of Madame Foucard, Monsieur de Montigny is representing me,' he announced.

The Commissaire looked him over. More than ever, Hélory resembled a weasel. 'Do you need legal representation, Monsieur?' he enquired coldly.

Sharp black eyes gleamed at him. 'I don't know. I'm a cautious chap and I've always kept my nose clean. I can't believe Marguerite would disappear of her own accord. I don't like it.'

'What d'you fear has happened to her?'

'They've got her.'

Orloff's face showed none of his surprise. 'You think she's been abducted? By whom?'

'Luc's friends, of course,' Hélory replied with a touch of scorn. 'I don't believe in mixing it with the cloak-and-dagger guys. And so I told her, but would she ever listen?'

'I'm surprised, Monsieur, that you know what Luc's duties were.'

'Wives have a right to know.'

'Agreed, but they should know better than blab it around. In any case, I understood he had retired from active service.'

'That was just a tale. Why else would he have been going away for six months, if he wasn't back on the job?'

Bernard de Montigny frowned and opened his mouth to speak, but the Commissaire stopped him with a slight shake of the head. 'How d'you know, Monsieur? If he were going back to his work, he'd hardly broadcast the fact.'

'Marguerite'd arranged to live in his house while he was away.'

'Madame Foucard never said a word to me about this,' Bernard said in a strangled voice.

'It was none of your business, Maître, until something happened to her,' Hélory replied sharply.

Orloff intervened. 'Apart from your general suspicion of Naval Intelligence, what are your grounds for belief that Madame Foucard has been abducted by its agents?'

'Knew too much, didn't she?'

'I don't know. You tell me.'

'No bloody fear! Look Commissaire, can you fix up a meeting? There must be some way of convincing them that Marguerite and I don't give a damn about their operations.'

'As long as they don't interfere with yours?' Orloff suggested.

'Something like that,' Hélory agreed. 'Tell them Marguerite and I know how to keep our mouths shut,' he added and proceeded to demonstrate the fact, resisting all manner of probing from that moment on.

Marcel Landais presented himself at the prison at an early hour. He was feeling peeved. He had no idea what the police were doing. It had to be something new, with his client taken out of his reach for hours on end the previous day. Whatever Commissaire Orloff was up to, he was sure it would upset his own plans. He could see his big chance drifting out of his grasp.

As he waited for the wardress to bring Christine, he pondered the problem. No one, he resolved grimly, was going to chisel him.

Her arrival scattered his ideas. Landais found it difficult to credit that a person could change so markedly overnight. He studied her face, unexpectedly appreciating the nature of her beauty – good bone structure and perfect skin, naturally pale in contrast with her hair, all the same as yesterday, but lit now with an inner glow kindled by the expulsion of fear, and fed by the serenity of one who has survived an ordeal.

For the first time, Marcel Landais looked at his client as a man looks at a woman . . . He found it highly disconcerting, aware of a reversal of roles, and nervous in the face of her calm.

'Why were you taken to Lannion yesterday?' he barked, in the hope of regaining the upper hand.

'To assist enquiries,' she said, with a smile.

111

He shot her a suspicious glance. Was she mocking him? 'Such as what? Kindly remember I'm on your side, Mademoiselle, while the police are not.'

At the back of his mind a nasty little voice gave him the lie, reminding him that in all his life he'd been on no one's side but his own. Christine's eyes lit with amusement and, for one horrible moment, he saw his ambitions in a new light.

'Commissaire Orloff is very thorough. He checks every detail. With unexpected results, Monsieur. He made me remember why I went round to the kitchen door.'

His eyes narrowed. 'Why did you?'

'Because I thought there was someone in the house.'

Landais threw himself back in his chair. 'What nonsense is this? You're making it up.'

Christine shook her head. 'Oh, no. The Commissaire took me over what I did that day, step by step, at the house itself. It was like living that day over again.'

'That doesn't seem to be bothering you.'

'Not any more. It wasn't easy, putting myself back to that morning, but once I'd faced it, I felt – how can I describe it? – released, like waking from a nightmare.'

'Let me remind you that you're in prison, facing serious charges,' he said grimly.

A wonderful smile swept over her mouth, shaking his resistance. 'Not for much longer, Monsieur. I'm certain of that.'

'You have so much faith in Commissaire Orloff?'

'Yes, I have.'

He seized on the admission, summoning up his resources for one last stand on his preconceived ideas. 'Then you're a fool, Mademoiselle. You and your father.'

The colour ebbed out of her face. 'What about my father?'

'If I'm able to put two and two together, so will others, and then the fat will be in the fire. Your father took a few days' leave. A couple of minutes' enquiry at the railway station at Guingamp confirmed my suspicion that he had gone to Paris. Then, out of the blue, Orloff appeared. Your father had gone to beg him to come to your assistance, hadn't he?'

Christine gazed at him coolly. 'I didn't suspect you of being so imaginative, Monsieur.'

Landais had to admire her poise and courage – the Brigadier

was lucky to have such a daughter, it would be no fault of hers if the rumour got out – but he was not yet ready to surrender. 'Orloff is here for his own ends, Mademoiselle, no matter what tale he has told you.'

At that she smiled. 'You can't know the Commissaire very well. He hasn't told me anything. He's a hard man, but he's digging about when everyone else wants the case closed. Whatever he finds will be brought into the light of day. That's all I need.'

'Ridiculous!' Landais gasped, still struggling, but more feebly.

The smile turned into a laugh. 'You must know the Commissaire's reputation: neither fear nor favour moves him. And he doesn't miss the smallest thing. He'll find Luc's murderer. Look how he's dug out my memory.'

Marcel Landais abandoned an untenable position. There was no way he could expect this fine creature to settle for less than acquittal – and he would have to fight for her, tooth and nail, if necessary.

'How sure are you that there was someone else in the house?'

'I can't say I saw anyone. I think I heard some movement.'

Landais sighed. 'That's hardly the sort of evidence to stand up in court. There's nothing to say it wasn't Luc himself.'

'It didn't take me long to walk round the side of the house, not time enough for someone to strike him down and escape through the kitchen door before I reached it.'

'That's Orloff's opinion?'

'I gather he deduces there was another person in the house. There's some question about the amount of sand walked into the kitchen. We retraced my steps all the way, and then he took my shoes for examination.'

'That sounds more likely,' said Landais brightly. 'Laboratory reports make a good impression in court.' A thought struck him, surprising him with a sharp pang of some emotion. 'If the murderer was in the house when you arrived, you may have had a narrow escape yourself. Killers don't like to be caught in the act.'

Christine bit her lip. 'I hadn't thought of that.' Then her face cleared. 'How idiotic! All these weeks I've been wishing I were dead, and now I see that I might have been, I'm so glad to be alive.'

'That's a healthy sign,' Landais heard himself say, and wondered what possessed him. 'Have you thought about the identity of the murderer?' he demanded sharply, to recover himself.

'Of course I have. I knew *I* hadn't done it.'

'And?'

She shook her head. 'Zilch. Even to get myself off the hook I can't point the finger at a soul. I've thought and thought, but there doesn't seem to be *anyone*. Yet it can't have been a stranger. Luc wouldn't have let in a person he didn't know.'

'You're sure of that?'

'Quite. I suppose he was a bit secretive,' she went on slowly. 'He never talked about himself, or his past life, or even his future. Only about the here and now.'

Landais had no wish to indulge in idle speculation over the dead man's past and whatever old evils might lurk in it. 'Who inherits?' he demanded, going for the obvious.

'Luc mentioned some charity.'

He was disappointed. He would have enjoyed pinning the crime on to one of the Plouviez clan. It would not make up for missing his grand opportunity to impress in court, but rankling slights would be avenged. 'Not the family? That's a pity. They're a pushy lot. I wonder Tremerrec's still big enough to hold them. Marrying into the Tremels was quite a step up for an obscure provincial family. The *dot* must have been sizeable, especially for a girl, ugly and past thirty at the time, I'm told.'

Christine giggled. 'I never thought I'd be sorry for Sacha's Aunt Simone. How awful to have to buy a husband.'

'You don't know it applies to you, too, Mademoiselle?'

She stared. 'I'd need a dowry? Not these days, Monsieur.'

'You do if you're going to marry into that sort of circle. Marriage contracts need cash. Didn't you realise Sacha would never have been allowed to marry you? How far had that *affaire* gone before you took up with Luc Plouviez?'

Colour rushed up into her face and her eyes flashed. 'Monsieur, I find that offensive. As far as I was concerned, there was never any question of marriage. We were friends, nothing more.'

The girl was more than just beautiful, she was magnificent. Marcel Landais was obliged to take a grip on himself.

'Did Sacha agree with you?'

Reluctantly, she shook her head.

'There you are, then. Sacha Plouviez could have been driven

to desperation by jealousy and frustration. Denied having you for himself, isn't it possible that he was determined his cousin Luc shouldn't have you?'

'But Luc had sent me away. And Sacha knew perfectly well that I cared for him only as a friend.'

'I admire you for defending the lad. But you hadn't gone back to him, had you? Sacha had met La Foucard. I doubt if he's blind or stupid. One glimpse would convince him that that "engagement" reeked. He'd know Luc would come after you again, once he'd rid himself of that woman and whatever foolish promise she'd extracted from him.'

Landais was amazed at himself. All disappointment vanished as he perceived a better alternative to grandstanding in court. What if he could beat Commissaire Orloff at his own game and be the first to uncover the murderer? That would set him up for life in Tremerrec, and surely Christine would be grateful. Ambition dictated that he should marry into an ancient Breton family, and what did it matter if the prospective bride would not bring him a sou?

The Plouviez family arrived in force: Sacha, Anatole, Simone Tremel and a thin, faded woman who turned out to be Anatole's wife, Yvonne. Grimly, the Commissaire looked them over, then broke up the united front. The two women were handed over to Inspector Durieux, while Orloff kept Sacha and his father for himself.

That morning, Anatole Plouviez was a worried man. 'Could I have a word with you in private, Commissaire?' he asked, casting an uneasy glance at his son.

'Certainly, when I have finished with Sacha,' Orloff replied blandly.

It was not what Anatole wanted, but he was in no position to argue. 'May I sit in on the interrogation?' he went on in unnatural humility. 'As his legal representative, of course.'

'I don't want him interfering,' Sacha burst out. 'I didn't kill Luc and I've nothing to hide.'

'Don't play the fool,' his father snapped back, irritation restoring him to something approaching his normal manner.

'Good advice, Monsieur,' Orloff cut in. 'Very well, you may stay, but since, at this stage, your son does not wish you to act for him, please keep quiet. Now, Sacha, you appear to have had more contact with Luc Plouviez than any other member of the family. You took him sailing?'

'That's right. Most weekends, until – ' the young man broke off, biting his lip.

'Until when?'

Sacha heaved a sigh. 'Until that row with Christine.'

'Which was after Madame Tremel's visit on July 14th. How long after?'

'The next day. Up till then, I hadn't realised – ' he gulped. 'I was a blind fool. I knew Christine liked Luc – so did I, he was great company – but it never occurred to me that she was in love with him, not until Aunt Simone came along, breathing fire.'

'It was a big shock to you?'

'I thought the world had come to an end. But I only wanted her to be happy. I didn't want Luc to muck about with her. I told you last night that's why I went to see him. But I never got past Christine. I lost them both,' Sacha went on, with a catch in his voice. 'When he sent her away, she wouldn't let me come near her, and then someone murdered Luc. But it wasn't Christine.'

Anatole stirred restlessly, but with Orloff's eyes upon him he held his peace.

'I'm hunting that murderer,' the Commissaire said in a deadly tone. 'You had a motive – jealousy – so let's examine your opportunity.'

'You said yourself I hadn't an alibi,' Sacha pointed out. 'I can't expect you to take my word for it. Are you arresting me?'

'All in good time. Let's find out exactly what happened on the morning of August 15th.' Orloff glanced at Anatole. 'This might as well be a combined effort, Monsieur. What were the arrangements for your reunion?'

'We have a routine, Commissaire,' Anatole told him. 'My sister and her family arrive about nine thirty – '

'From Rennes? They must make an early start.'

'They drive over the day before,' Sacha put in. 'Thank God, they don't stay with us, even though they collar my boat.'

His father glared at him. 'They go to the aunts, two very old ladies, my grandfather's younger sisters, at La Roche Blanche, and bring them over to us for the day.'

'Did the Tremels arrive on time?'

116

The memory appeared sour to Anatole. 'Certainly,' he grunted. 'My sister's a punctual person.'

Orloff could believe it. Simone Tremel would dragoon her family even on holiday. 'What went wrong?'

Father and son exchanged glances.

'It was my fault,' Sacha admitted. 'I got up late.'

'You were just having breakfast when our visitors arrived,' Anatole reminded him.

'And you were chewing my ear off. Aunt Simone had to chip in too, didn't she?' He turned back to Orloff. 'There wasn't much I could do but split.'

'Have you remembered what route you took?'

Sacha hesitated. 'I passed through Plougrescant.'

Anatole let out a hiss of exasperation. 'You'd have done better to have forgotten that altogether.'

'I didn't go on to Devil's Bay, Papa. I wish I had.'

His father appealed to Orloff. 'I know this looks bad, but my son isn't entirely a fool. He didn't have to admit he was so near to Devil's Bay.'

'I shall need a description of your car and its registration number, Sacha,' the Commissaire replied. 'Try to recall where else you went. What time did you return home?'

'About half past twelve.'

'Later. We were all on board the yacht and waiting for you,' said Anatole, in sharp displeasure. 'If you get out of this mess, perhaps you'll pay a little more attention to me.'

'And perhaps you'll stop trying to mould me into your own image,' Sacha retorted. 'Why can't you let me do what I want?'

Anatole clenched his teeth. 'When this is all over, I'll wash my hands of you, I promise you.'

'Suits me, Papa. Any time you like.'

Orloff interrupted the quarrel. 'You may fight this out afterwards, Messieurs. You, Sacha, are going to be put into a quiet room, with pencil and paper, so that you may do your best to reconstruct your drive that morning, while I talk to your father.'

Anatole said nothing until the door had closed behind the young man. Then he burst out, 'This is a nightmare, Commissaire. It never occurred to me that Christine might not be the killer.'

Orloff gazed at him. For once, the man had lost his bombast. Those words came from the heart. 'Consider it seriously now, Monsieur. I'm looking elsewhere for the murderer. You understand that I must examine the position of the dead man's family first.'

'But we are not the principal heirs. The property and the money go to charity.'

'Not so the contents of the house.'

'Ah, but that has to be shared out between all surviving members of our family, no less than forty-two persons, Commissaire,' Anatole said smugly.

Orloff pushed a slip of paper across the desk. 'A valuer has been in there this morning. That is the rough figure. At auction the stuff might fetch a good deal more. It's a fine collection of oriental art.'

Anatole's eyes bulged. 'So much? It's a fortune.'

For one who would be a beneficiary, he did not sound over-joyed.

'Many a person has been killed for far less than one share in that.'

Anatole groaned. 'I suppose you'll take us all apart.'

'If I have to, Monsieur. Let's start with you.'

Sweat broke out on the man's forehead. He fumbled for a handkerchief to wipe it away. 'You may count on my cooperation,' he said, summoning up courage.

'Thank you. What were your movements on the morning of the murder? Yesterday evening, you were out looking for your son after a quarrel. Is that what you usually do?'

Anatole mopped his face again. 'Yes, I'm always ashamed when I've let fly at Sacha. The boy's a disappointment to me. It isn't that he's stupid, he just doesn't want to achieve any-thing.'

'You went after him that morning?'

'As far as Tremerrec. I thought he'd gone to meet his friends, not the sort of people I like my son to associate with, they hang out in a bar on the wharf. He wasn't there.'

'Did you go in and ask for him?'

'To be laughed at as an old fusspot? I've learnt my lesson over that, Commissaire. His car would've been out front if he were there. It wasn't.'

'What did you do then?'

'I sat in the car for a while, in case he turned up. I waited until

118

the Cathedral bell had stopped tolling, then I gave up and went to Mass.'

'Did you sit with your family?'

'Not a chance, the place was crammed. I stood near the back in case Sacha appeared.'

'Did he?'

Anatole shook his head. 'There wasn't a sign of him until he turned up at home.'

'What time did the Mass end?'

'Shortly after eleven thirty.'

'Did you see people whom you knew, friends, and acquaintances?'

'Naturally. I passed the time of day with several people in the square.'

'I meant, inside the Cathedral. Can anyone of your acquaintance vouch for your presence?'

Anatole swallowed. 'I was in a crowd of visitors. Latecomers, like me.'

'So, in effect, there is no one who can swear you were in the places you claim to have been from, say, ten o'clock until eleven thirty. Luc Plouviez was murdered not later than eleven. How long does it take to drive from Tremerrec to Devil's Bay? Twenty minutes, at the outside. Time enough for you to get back to the Cathedral and mingle with the crowd coming out, with no one to know you hadn't been there for the Mass.'

His witness gaped at him, appalled, then, visibly, took a grip on himself. 'Murders require motives, Commissaire. I'm not desperate for my share of Luc's possessions.'

'You support quite a lifestyle. A large house, cars, a yacht, expensive clothes, personal jewellery,' said Orloff, gazing at the gold ring adorning one stubby hand and the star sapphire on the other.

Dusky colour suffused Anatole's face, as he bit back a protest at the offensive question. 'My financial position is sound,' he grated. 'You may examine it at your will.'

'I heard a rumour of debts.'

'Malicious rubbish.'

'It was a matter of years ago,' Orloff conceded.

'Twenty, at least. Folks round here have long memories,' said Anatole grimly. 'It's true we went through a bad patch a long time ago. My father made a fool of himself in later life. He took to gambling, which was bad news for the business when word got round, as it was bound to do. So we persuaded him to retire. I cleaned up that mess and I've had to fight hard to attain my present position. I worked my butt off for my family's sake, Commissaire, but I doubt if the gossips told you that. There's always someone who envies another's success, and I admit I've made a few enemies on my way up.'

'You saw Luc last in May. Any communication after that?'

Anatole shot him a wary glance. 'I had a phone call from him the Saturday before he was killed.'

'What about?'

'Business matters. Luc didn't give a toss for the family, but he knew I'd managed his affairs very well for him. I carried on handling routine matters for him, bills and the like. He needed to adjust the arrangements.'

'Because he was going away?'

Anatole was surprised. 'You knew about that?'

'I make it my business to gather all possible information,' Orloff said sharply. 'Did he say where he was going?'

'He told me Cyprus. To spend the winter in a warmer climate.'

'Leaving his fiancée to mind the house? I wonder why he didn't think of taking her with him?' the Commissaire said provocatively.

'I wasn't in Luc's confidence,' Anatole replied with a wry twist of the lips. 'If he was fool enough to leave a handsome woman to her own devices, that was his affair. At least it was going to save us the trouble of packing up the furniture again. That house is too isolated to be left with everything in it.'

'What will happen to it now? Will the charity put it on the market?'

Anatole looked taken aback by the sudden question. 'I'm not in a position to say.'

'Have you been approached about it, since the murder, that is?'

'Madame Foucard expressed an interest.'

'D'you know why?'

Anatole shrugged. 'Sentimental attachment, perhaps.'

Orloff could imagine nothing less likely. It appeared to have no bearing on the investigation, but the lady's choice of an ugly and inconvenient house was the sort of detail which bothered him. Marguerite Foucard had to be found as quickly as possible.

'Has her offer been accepted?'

Anatole took refuge in legal formality. 'It will be months before the charity will be free to dispose of it, as I'm sure you appreciate, Commissaire.'

Fired with his latest idea, Marcel Landais drove over to Devil's Bay. Detection, he surmised, had to begin with the corpse, and, in its absence, the place where the murder was done. Not being devoted to the great outdoors, he had never visited this spot. On a dull, wet day, it looked less than attractive, the rainclouds providing a menacing backdrop to the tumbled rocks. The Plouviez house, gaunt and forbidding, was visible but inaccessible, with a bored gendarme guarding the track leading to it. There was not another soul in sight.

As a scene-of-crime, it told Landais nothing at all.

Refusing to allow himself to be depressed, he drove round to the other side of the house, approaching from the lane to the farm. Slowly he drove over the potholed and muddy surface, looking for some place to park. There was only one, a spot where the hedges sloped away at the mouth of a track. Someone else was there before him. A car with Paris number plates stood to one side, leaving barely enough room for another. Some muckraking journalist, Landais thought darkly, wedging in beside it.

On foot he made his way up the lane, deploring mudsplashes on his highly-polished shoes, and passed the other entrance to the Plouviez house closed by a police tape. From it, there was a clear view of the front where a gendarme was taking shelter from the rain in the porch at the bottom of the tower. Beyond the house towered the eroded cliff which concealed The Chasm. Landais paused, making a mental picture of the girl coming down over the rocks, her long skirts billowing in the wind, and her loops of lace startling white against the raven hair.

A movement in the porch brought him out of this delicious reverie, as he discovered a hard and inquisitive police stare riveted on him. He moved away hurriedly, careless of the mud.

The lane took a sharp turn away from the house, and the tarmac surface finished, giving way to a cinder track. Sighting grey stone buildings in the distance, Landais trudged on between the fields, wondering how far it might be to the farm, and asking himself if he should go back for the car. He drew level with a neat building of cement blocks, whose purpose he could not imagine, marooned as it was in a sea of cabbages.

Suddenly, he became aware of voices, of a man and a woman, raised in argument. He halted. It was all very bizarre to be alone in a dreary agricultural landscape, yet eavesdropping on a quarrel. Then a small, elderly woman shot out from behind the concrete hut, stopping short when she caught sight of Landais twenty yards away.

'Who are you and what d'you want?' she demanded.

He put on a winning smile. 'Madame Basret? My card,' he said, producing the same with a flourish. 'I am looking after Christine Kergrist's interests.'

Janine picked her way between the rows of cabbages. She scrutinised the card. 'At least you're not a reporter,' she conceded.

Landais thought he spotted an opportunity to ingratiate himself. 'I'm sure those fellows are a great nuisance, Madame. I saw the car.'

Alarm flooded into her face. 'What's that?'

'The one in the lane, Madame. I parked beside it.'

'I won't have people snooping round here,' she declared. 'I wonder where he is? Show me that car.'

Landais humoured her, though he thought it unlikely that the owner would have returned in the short time since he had parked beside it. But this woman could be a valuable source of information for him. Together they tramped down the lane. The first glimpse of the car drew an exclamation of annoyance from Janine.

'That pesky woman again!'

'You recognise that car?'

'Indeed, I do. It belongs to Madame Foucard. She must be at the house.'

She turned on her heel and marched back. Landais close behind. She halted at the police cordon.

'Hey, you!' she yelled at the *gendarme* in the porch. 'Tell La Foucard to shift her car off our land.'

He came at a run. 'What's the matter?'

Janine demanded to know if he had ears and repeated the message.

'Are you sure it's her car, Madame? Where is it?'

'See for yourself.'

The man was running in the direction she pointed. Janine and Landais came up with him as he was calling in on his personal radio. He gazed at them both with deep suspicion.

'How long has this vehicle been here?'

Janine sniffed. 'How should I know? This is the first time I've been down the lane today.'

'I've only just arrived,' Landais said hastily.

'Is that your car, Monsieur? Drive it round to the beach and wait there. You go with him, please, Madame.'

'What's all the fuss about?' she grumbled as she settled herself in the passenger seat.

'There's a call out for Marguerite Foucard. Nobody knows where she is,' the *gendarme* told him, shutting the door he had held open for Janine.

'She can't be far away,' said Landais. 'Could she be at the farm?'

'No, she couldn't,' Janine snapped back. 'That one wouldn't have walked all the way up the lane, and my son would have pitched her straight out if she had. He's work to do.'

Under the direction of the policeman, they parked at the end of the causeway. Landais gazed up at the rock formation towering over them.

'This is a strange place,' he remarked. 'Where's The Chasm?'

'Right in front of us. You have to climb up there to see it.'

Instantly he was out of the car. 'I might as well take a look while we're waiting.'

The path was steeper than he anticipated. Panting, he stepped gingerly to the edge and peered over. He had expected vicious rocks and angry water. A body clad in a torn black and orange frock was an undesirable extra.

Chapter 10

Death was unkind to Marguerite Foucard, stripping off her careful artwork to reveal a sagging body, a sack of flaccid skin in a spreading pool of seawater. Blank eyes stared out of an ageing face framed by hair hanging wet and straight, revealing grey roots.

Orloff stared down at her, faintly regretful. Whatever her faults, she had enjoyed her life.

'She's a mess, Commissaire,' said the Medical Officer, scrambling to his feet, his examination finished. 'Bodies usually are, when they've been in The Chasm. It isn't the way I'd choose to do myself in.'

'Have you seen many?'

'Suicides? Five or six, I suppose, over the past ten years. Why?'

'I was wondering if they habitually end up in the same position at the bottom.'

'I can't say for sure, Commissaire,' the doctor replied cheerfully. 'You'd best ask Henri Drouon. He's the one who fishes them out.'

Orloff glanced down at the beach, crowded now with police vehicles. On the other side of the causeway a cordon held back spectators, who seemed to have sprung up from nowhere despite the persistent drizzle blowing in off the sea. He picked out a man standing beside a battered truck inside the tape, but taking no part in the activity.

'That's him,' the doctor added, following the Commissaire's gaze. 'He deals with suicides and washed-up bodies. It's a great work of charity, but it isn't everyone who could stomach it. Henri's an old Resistance fighter. I expect he's seen worse than anything the sea can do.'

Orloff turned back to the corpse. 'How long has she been dead?'

'Hours. Overnight, at a guess. There are bruises and scratches all over her. They'll take a bit of sorting out. I'd say she went in head first. Okay to send her to the morgue?'

The Commissaire nodded, and the body was enveloped in a plastic bag to be carried down to the mortuary van at the bottom of the cliff.

'I don't think I can buy suicide,' said Inspector Durieux. 'Not with that woman. Can you imagine her killing herself?'

Orloff permitted himself a bleak smile. 'Hardly. The question is: was she pushed, or did she miss her footing? She was last seen about eight o'clock yesterday evening, leaving the hotel. Since she had an appointment later with Hélory, the inference is that she was on urgent business which she thought she could do before he arrived. How long has that car been in the lane?'

'Could be overnight. There's a dry patch under it. The rain didn't begin until about five this morning.'

'Didn't the farmer see it?'

Durieux shook his head. 'Apparently not. The old girl says her son's fed up with reporters blocking the lane. He'd have raised Cain if he'd seen it. He and his wife left around six yesterday, driving to Carnac for a funeral this morning. His mother stayed behind to mind the farm. She says she went to bed at nine. I doubt if sounds would carry that far, Commissaire, not to be able to pinpoint, that is. The farm's way up that lane.'

'What about the guards at the house? Didn't they hear anything?'

'The devils were playing cards all evening.'

'Even so, they'd have heard a scream,' Orloff pointed out.

'Suicides don't yell. Or do they? But people falling by accident do. So would someone being pushed.'

'Not if they were being thrown in unconscious or already dead.'

'I wouldn't fancy carrying La Foucard up here,' said Durieux. 'She'd weigh.'

'So she would. I wonder how it was done,' Orloff murmured, starting down the steep path.

Janine Basret and Marcel Landais had been taken into the Plouviez house to await the Commissaire. This pleased the lawyer, his sharp eyes darting everywhere to take in as much as possible in the time available. His expectations received a sudden check

125

when the pair were bundled into the kitchen, Janine grumbling fiercely about being kept from her work.

Orloff was curious to meet Christine's lawyer, having heard the opinion of Brigadier Kergrist. He detected an interesting change of stance.

'What were you doing here, Monsieur?' he enquired.

'Trying to serve my client's best interests,' Landais replied challengingly, to cover a certain dismay at being so dwarfed by the immense size of the Commissaire.

'I'm glad to hear it, Monsieur. You've done me a service, too. I was looking for Madame Foucard. Did you know her?'

'She had been pointed out to me. A very striking lady. I recognised her dress,' he admitted, with a shudder. 'Do you need me any more?'

'Not for the moment, Monsieur. You're free to leave. With my thanks.'

Landais made for the door, Janine going before him.

Orloff called her back. 'Another little moment, Madame, if you please.'

'I've nothing more to tell you,' she snapped, blocking the lawyer's exit. 'I haven't seen hide nor hair of that woman for weeks. My son and his wife are away. I must get back. I'm alone at the farm.'

'But you were talking to someone. Arguing,' Landais exclaimed.

All colour drained out of Janine's face. She stared at him in consternation. 'It's not true,' she croaked.

'You were at that concrete hut,' Landais insisted, but Orloff held up a warning hand.

'It's no good, Madame,' he said, not unkindly. 'You can't hope to shield Pierre for ever. He has disappeared from his job and his lodgings in Brest. I knew you must be hiding him. You have him in this hut?'

'It's the pumphouse for the water for this place,' she said wretchedly. 'Don't be hard on him, Commissaire. He's a fool to himself. But I'll swear he isn't a murderer.'

'That remains to be seen, Madame,' Orloff replied, and stalked off to send Inspector Durieux to pick up Pierre Basret.

On the beach the crowd had thinned, but Henri Drouon was still there, in case he was needed. The approach of the Commissaire did not appear to impress him. He did not budge from his position, half-perched on the bonnet of his truck, calmly smoking his pipe. The old farmer's eyes, bright and alert, sized up the policeman, reserving judgment.

Orloff came to a halt in front of him, liking what he saw: a chunky solid Breton, firm of mouth and straight of glance, a good ally, a bad enemy.

'Monsieur Drouon? I'm acquainted with one of your daughters, Madame Kergrist. Also Mademoiselle Kergrist.'

The old man nodded. 'You would be. I'm proud of Christine. She's a clever girl. And she isn't a murderess,' he added, defiantly, tapping out his pipe.

'I'm beginning to think you might be right, but don't quote me.'

In his surprise Drouon dropped his pipe and let it lie on the pebbles. 'Then what's she doing in prison?'

'I need hard evidence to convince the *juge d'instruction*.'

'Is there anything I can do?'

'Perhaps. There's so much I don't know about that house and the people who lived in it.'

Drouon followed his gaze. 'It should never have been built. Brave men died there.'

'I'm told you were campaigning for a memorial.'

Drouon snorted. 'Fat chance we had of extracting that bit of land out of Papa Basret, Janine's husband. He's dead now. A proper skinflint, he was. There wasn't anything he could do with the land, either. It was no good for farming, covered with great chunks of rubble.'

'The old gun emplacement?'

'That's right. My unit had instructions from London to blow it up, to create a diversion in advance of the Allied invasion. All we could do was disable it, at the cost of half of our men. Even after the war, the Army couldn't destroy it completely. The Germans built to last,' he added grimly. 'Some of them are still down there, where the charges we laid sealed them in.'

Orloff frowned. 'You didn't get the bodies out?'

'The Boches weren't all that popular round here immediately after the Liberation. Too many people had suffered. Those guys were conveniently forgotten. But later, I began to feel uneasy about them. By that time there was no way they could be got out. There's tons of concrete on top of them. That's when I started agitating for a memorial for the fallen, ours and theirs. By rights, it should have been scheduled as a war grave.'

'You didn't succeed?'

'Not a hope. Basret was a cunning old devil. He pulled strings and persuaded people there weren't any bodies down there. He even managed to open up one of the tunnels to show but, of course, the bodies were way down. Folks were only too glad to believe him. No one minded when Emile Plouviez came along and bought the site. I could've told him it'd only bring him ill luck. It's a bad place.'

'You'd know him, naturally, being a neighbour.'

'He wasn't a sociable man,' Drouon grunted. 'A right eccentric, was Emile. He and that man of his set out to build the place themselves. Then the tower fell down when it was half built. He had to call in a builder after that, and groused at every bill.'

'He was reputed to be fabulously rich.'

Drouon laughed. 'It's the ones that have the most that spend least, Commissaire. If Emile Plouviez really was sitting on a heap of money, that's the way he wanted it. He wouldn't have a telephone or a car, and he never entertained. All he did was go sailing in a little old boat. And in the end the sea got him.'

'You dealt with the body that was washed up?'

'It was young Paul. Emile and his man didn't come ashore.'

'Was that unusual?'

'It's a nasty bit of sea hereabouts. Bodies come in pretty quick or they don't come at all. I was hoping the house might be pulled down after that. There was some talk about a syndicate buying it, to demolish and restore this stretch of the coast to its natural state. It didn't come to anything.'

'Luc decided to keep it.'

Drouon shrugged. 'I can't think why. He never came near it until his accident. It's a pity he didn't stay away altogether.' He stooped and picked up his pipe. 'This place wasn't named Devil's Bay for nothing. It's seen a lot of death: the war, suicides, wrecks, and now murder. Did that woman do it, Commissaire, then do herself in?'

'I very much doubt it, Monsieur.'

Inspector Durieux surprised Pierre Basret asleep on the camp bed his mother had rigged up for him in the confined space of the pumphouse. On the floor beside it was a tray of dirty dinner dishes and an empty bottle that had contained cheap wine. He raised a tousled head in response to the curt summons back into the waking world, peering out of one bleary eye at the figures standing in the doorway of the windowless hut.

'Wassermarrer?' he muttered.

'Out,' Durieux commanded. '*Police judiciaire.*'

The words worked wonders. Pierre shot out of his blanket, staring wildly at the Inspector and his men.

'What's up? Can't a man take a holiday on his brother's farm?' he demanded with an attempt at bluster.

'Some guestroom,' Durieux remarked. 'Your brother doesn't know you're here, does he? Up you get. You're wanted for questioning in connection with the murder of Luc Plouviez.'

'*Luc?*' Pierre shouted, the onset of panic clearing his head. 'You can't pin that on me.'

The Inspector stepped aside for his men to enter the hut. There was a brief struggle before the man was hauled out. By the light of day, Pierre was revealed as a stocky individual with a beer-belly, a pasty complexion and thinning black hair. Bloodshot eyes stared from under shaggy brows. He was fully dressed and gave off a mixture of unpleasant odours.

He lunged forward a couple of paces in Durieux's direction, but was held back. 'Have a heart, Inspector, I'm only a poor bugger that doesn't know how to earn a living.'

'You can cut that out,' Durieux replied. 'You've just done a stretch for robbery with violence.'

'I wouldn't *kill* anyone.'

'You damned near finished off one of your victims last time. All right, lads, take him away. And clean him up a bit before the Commissaire sees him.'

Waiting in the back of the Inspector's car, Janine Basret burst into tears at the sight of her favourite child borne away in a police van. She jumped out and clutched Durieux's arm.

'Pierre isn't a bad boy, Inspector, only foolish. He wouldn't harm a fly.'

He gazed down at her in mingled pity and exasperation. 'Don't deceive yourself any more, Madame. You can't protect him for ever. He's a man now, not a child. If you want to help him, tell us the truth.'

She turned away abruptly. 'I've nothing to say.'

'Why? Because he was hiding out in that hut when Luc was killed?'

Her shoulders sagged under an invisible burden. 'I knew you'd think the worst. He'd just come out of prison, and he hadn't anywhere to go.'

'When did he arrive?'

'On August 3rd or 4th.'

'Until when?'

'The 16th. He went to Brest. I've a cousin there who promised him a job. He seemed to be settling down. I was afraid it might be too good to be true.'

'When did he come back?'

'Three days ago. He said he needed a rest. I suppose that isn't the truth, either. It hasn't taken him long to get into bad company.'

'His sort gravitate to it, Madame.'

'But it doesn't make him a murderer,' Janine declared, with a resurgence of maternal faith.

'It might, if he was up to his old tricks, and Luc Plouviez found him searching for Uncle Emile's treasure.'

'That old tale!' she exclaimed scornfully. 'That's a load of rubbish. I know every nook and cranny of that house. There's nowhere to hide anything.'

'Ah, but does Pierre still believe the treasure exists? That's the point, Madame. Judging by his record, he'd lash out with the nearest weapon if caught breaking in.'

The Commissaire had an unexpected visitor, an imposing man with silver-grey hair and a quietly intimidating manner which sent a police officer scurrying into Orloff's office. He handed over a plain envelope. The Commissaire opened it and drew out a card announcing the presence of Admiral Raoul Medina (Retired).

He was wearing civilian clothes and carrying a briefcase like any businessman, but the Commissaire was not deceived. This was no beached sailor.

'I was expecting a visit from someone in your department,' he said coolly.

The Admiral sat down. 'We've been keeping a watching brief,

130

Commissaire. I was a little concerned about the case being reopened.'

Orloff was not prepared to accept that. 'Did any old scapegoat suit you, Admiral?'

Medina frowned slightly. 'There are security angles.'

'So I supposed. The cover story about being blown up in an accident during gunnery practice didn't bear investigation, but once you'd put it out, you were stuck with it.'

'We'd no idea anyone would wish to question it,' his visitor said dismissively. 'It's not important.'

'I may need to know how Luc Plouviez was wounded.'

The Admiral stiffened, but Orloff swept on: 'I have to tell you that Marguerite Foucard was found dead today in suspicious circumstances. Was she one of your people, too?'

'Good God, no.'

'Yet she was connected with Luc Plouviez in some way which everyone seems to be at pains to keep quiet. I'm sure you know the inside story, Admiral.'

Medina thought for a moment. 'Luc was a good man,' he said carefully. 'Our own investigators satisfied me that his death had no connection with the work he was doing when he was so unfortunately put out of action. The reappearance of Madame Foucard in his life had given rise to a certain anxiety. There might be a breach of security somewhere.'

Orloff understood the position. 'I suggest we cooperate. I infer that La Foucard was involved in Luc's operations, probably inadvertently. I deduce that this took place in the Lebanon.'

· The Admiral was alarmed. 'This can't be discussed.'

'It has to be. Between you and me. I'm not prepared to sacrifice a young girl's future for a security cover-up. If the Lebanese connection has no bearing on the murder investigation, it can be kept quiet. But I need to know. Why else are you here, Admiral?'

Medina smiled faintly. 'I was warned you were a hard case, Commissaire, and I am aware of your security clearance. Very well. In confidentiality. Luc, as you have guessed, was on a mission in Beirut. He got caught in a faction fight. The house he was in was blown up by a shell, and Luc found himself in a cellar under a pile of debris. Madame Foucard was in the basement of the building next door. That had been reinforced for use as a shelter. Even so, the blast made a hole in the wall. She heard Luc groaning and rescued him.' He paused, then went on, 'She had some supplies, food, water, and a first-aid box. She kept him alive until they were found, days later.'

Orloff nodded. 'She was a tough lady. Yes, I can see her fighting off death as she had tackled other challenges. It isn't always the virtuous who show up best in a crisis.'

'So you know something of her?'

'Enough, Admiral. Do you know what she was doing in Lebanon?'

'She said she was visiting friends. That could be true,' Medina replied cautiously.

'There are friends and friends. Was her engagement to Luc Plouviez a stunt, I wonder?'

His visitor's face, always impassive, seemed turned to stone. 'I can't help you on that, Commissaire.'

Orloff did not believe him. He tried another tack. 'Luc wasn't "retired", was he? He was making arrangements to return to Cyprus.'

'To a desk job. He knew the eastern Mediterranean like the back of his hand. There's no secret about that.'

'Postponing his marriage, too, presumably?'

The Admiral looked displeased. 'I can't see that this has any bearing on your investigation, Commissaire.'

'No? Consider the position. It's clear to me that Luc Plouviez was your top man in that area, so invaluable that even disabled he was virtually indispensable. Marguerite Foucard had been around the Lebanon for a long time and must have had hundreds of contacts, some, regrettably, on the wrong side of the law. A useful source of information, but hardly a suitable wife for a member of your "family". If *she* had been killed first, I might even have suspected your people of having arranged it.'

There was a short silence, then Medina said crossly, 'I suppose we are both on the same side. You're quite right, I was bringing Luc back on duty before he was properly fit, in the hope of prising him out of La Foucard's grasp. Luc had made a foolish promise to her when they were stuck in that cellar; after all, she undoubtedly saved his life. He was a man of honour, Commissaire. When she turned up to hold him to his promise, he announced the engagement.'

'I'll accept that he meant it. What I can't swallow is that she did.'

'I agree. I toyed with the idea that she had had him killed once she had got hold of the house. It appeared that that was her objective, for some purpose of her own. But it seems he had left her no rights to it, so the theory doesn't hold water. Has she been murdered, too?'

'It's too early to say, but it looks like it. I shall be attending the post-mortem as soon as the pathologist arrives. Then I shall know for sure.'

The Admiral rose. 'I shall leave you to it, Commissaire. On a personal level,' he said, unexpectedly unbending, 'I'd like to see Luc's murderer brought to justice. He's a loss to me and to France.'

Identifying a corpse in the morgue was hardly Bernard de Montigny's idea of service to a client. Gloomily, he accepted it as his lot, comforted only by the greater distress of the dead woman's business partner. Jacques Hélory emerged in a state of near-collapse. Together, they faced the Commissaire.

'I've advised my client to explain to you the nature of his business relations with the late Madame Foucard,' Bernard announced crisply.

'Very wise,' Orloff commented. 'Monsieur Hélory, would you say Marguerite Foucard was the sort of person to commit suicide if circumstances threatened to overwhelm her?'

Hélory's face turned an even sicklier green. He shook his head unhappily.

'Was there anything in her dealings with you that might present her with – for example – insuperable financial difficulties?'

Another shake of the head. 'She'd got it all worked out,' he blurted.

'And what was this "it", Monsieur?'

Sweat broke out on Hélory's forehead. 'She was helping people.'

Orloff fixed a malevolent eye on him. 'I agree she rose to the occasion when Luc Plouviez was blown up, but please don't try to persuade me that Marguerite Foucard had turned over a new leaf altogether. I've a very good idea of her past history.'

Mystified, Bernard was staring, but Hélory understood all too well. 'You know what happened to Luc?' he gasped.

'I do. So let's take it from there. What was she doing in Beirut and whom was she "helping"?'

'Those poor buggers are up against it.'

'If by that you mean the inhabitants of the Lebanon, that's without question. She was doing business with them?'

'That's right. The idea was to build up bank balances abroad for them. For when they might have to leave in a hurry.'

'Now we're getting to it,' said Orloff with satisfaction. 'What was she doing?'

'Buying portable valuables, paying the money into numbered accounts.'

'Taking a percentage for herself?'

Hélory shook his head. 'Outright sales, Commissaire.'

'At rock-bottom prices.'

'There's nothing illegal in that,' Hélory protested. 'They could lose their possessions at any minute, and who was willing to buy them? Margot was taking all the risk. The agreed prices were paid into the bank accounts.'

'I suppose it's one step better than looting. Where are these goods?'

'In Cyprus, awaiting shipping. There were problems.'

'No doubt. To be brutally frank, Monsieur, all these valuable objects were smuggled out of the Lebanon into Cyprus, and would be smuggled out again and into France. I can envisage endless problems. Did Luc Plouviez know about this?'

'He saw some of the stuff,' Hélory admitted. 'That cellar of hers was stacked to the ceiling.'

'I begin to perceive daylight,' Orloff announced. 'La Foucard went in search of Luc because she was looking for a safe place to stash her booty. I imagine Luc had told her about his house during those long hours incarcerated under the debris. It would sound ideal to her, and the sight of it must have knocked her back. It's a gift to a smuggler of *objets d'art*. With Uncle Emile's collection already in place, a few additions to it would hardly be noticed, and the stuff could be brought in by sea in small boats.'

Hélory's unhappy face told him he was right on target, while Bernard shifted uneasily on his chair as his late client's illegal acts were exposed.

'She'd be obliged to marry the man, which must have been a slight disadvantage,' Orloff resumed. 'What had she told him?

134

That she was rescuing her family's treasures? I can't see Luc Plouviez standing for a smuggling racket.'

'I tried to warn her,' Hélory groaned.

'And what was your part in this scheme, Monsieur?'

Bernard intervened. 'I don't think my client should answer that immediately. May we confer?'

Hélory waved him aside. 'I don't mind telling the Commissaire. I hadn't done anything. You can't be had up for what you might do in the future. She wanted me to shift the stuff for her, a piece or two at a time.'

'What a very optimistic woman she was,' Orloff remarked. 'Sooner or later, Luc would be certain to find out what she was doing. From what I've learnt about him, he'd have hit the roof. Not a good start to a marriage.'

'Oh, that! To tell you the truth, Commissaire, I never thought she'd go through with it. Not when the crunch came. She only wanted to use the house.'

'She was trying to buy the place,' Bernard said. 'Now I understand why. She wouldn't have got it. Anatole Plouviez's after it himself, I'm told, to turn it into holiday flats.'

'Bizarre,' said Orloff. 'His own cousin was murdered there and he must have heard about the unknown number of dead Germans under the remains of the gun battery. One wonders what he would put in the brochure. Monsieur Hélory, what other little deals was Madame Foucard engaged in?'

The antique dealer's face betrayed nothing. 'None to my knowledge, but she had many interests. Commissaire, did someone push her into The Chasm?'

'If the post-mortem examination reveals that they did, I'll be looking at her associates. So far, I only have you, Monsieur.' Hélory looked alarmed, and Orloff went on, 'It would be helpful if you could recall the names of one or two others. I feel sure you've known Marguerite Foucard for a long time. Did she break her journey in Rennes on her way to Devil's Bay in August?'

'Does it matter?' Hélory gulped, startled at the sudden switch.

'It might, to you, Monsieur. Suppose the gallant Luc had discovered his fiancée's little money-making scheme. He would be an embarrassment to her and to you, perhaps to the point of requiring removal. Now, we know she couldn't have killed him, but she could have employed an agent. Can you account for your movements on the morning of August 15th?'

Hélory turned on Bernard. 'Do something, blast you!'

Orloff smiled his hunter's smile. 'Take Monsieur Hélory away and spell out his position to him, Maître. We'll continue this interview tomorrow.'

Minutes later, Inspector Durieux looked in to see if the Commissaire was alone. 'I've finished at the hotel. Drawn a blank, too. La Foucard was either one of the idle rich, or ultra discreet.'

Orloff was not surprised. 'Stick with discretion. That's how she survived so long.'

'There was one item of interest, though.' With a grin, Durieux laid a plastic bag on the desk. 'I'm damned if I know what to make of that.'

Inside it was a small blue bowl decorated with a design of white blossom. The last time they had seen it was on the table in the entrance hall of Luc Plouviez's house.

Chapter 11

Arriving at the *police judiciaire* offices, Inspector Durieux was surprised to find the Commissaire before him, despite being up until the small hours at the autopsy on Marguerite Foucard. He was busy writing up his notes taken at the mortuary.

'Sit down, Alain,' he invited. 'Have you your own notes?'

Durieux pulled them out of his pocket, feeling flattered. To be addressed by his Christian name felt like being given a medal. Suddenly, there came to him the answer to a problem which had lain at the back of his mind for days.

'Did Jules Kergrist appeal to you for help?'

The Commissaire glanced up from his work. 'That's an indiscreet question.'

'I wouldn't dream of asking it in public. He's an old friend.'

'I'm glad to hear that. Kergrist's a good cop and an even better father. He was taking a terrible risk. I doubt if I could have done much if Marguerite Foucard hadn't been involved, or Luc Plouviez hadn't been in Naval Intelligence. The combination was irresistible to my Minister.' He added a final sentence to his report, then put down his pen. 'We can't complain we've nothing to work on today.'

'The post-mortem didn't spring any surprises,' said Durieux. 'Suicide was a non-starter from the first, and I couldn't think of any reason for that woman to climb up to The Chasm in the dark, with fancy shoes on her feet.'

'Most unlikely,' Orloff agreed. 'In any case, there can be no argument now. La Foucard was killed by a series of blows to the back of the head. Where this happened, we don't yet know, but from the position of her car, it's reasonable to assume she was killed in the vicinity of Luc Plouviez's house, but not near enough for any sounds to have reached the ears of the guards inside.'

'I should have kept an outside watch overnight, too,' the Inspector muttered, furious with himself.

'Forget it. No one can foresee everything. The point of having guards was to prevent people entering the house. Muster every man you can for a fingertip search of the entire area. They're to look for the scene of the crime itself, and traces of any vehicles.'

Durieux made notes. 'The victim's own car is at the garage. I told them to look for traces of a passenger.'

'We have to cover that, but my own opinion is that she drove there alone. She was going to a rendezvous.'

'With a murderer. She must've been crazy.'

'Not La Foucard, Alain. Over-confident, probably, but not stupid.'

'You knew her better than I did,' he replied, clearly unconvinced.

'Indeed, I did. I found her a slippery customer. The only way she'd walk into a murder trap was if she didn't know there was any danger.'

'Her boyfriend had been chopped,' Durieux reminded him.

'That didn't appear to be bothering her overmuch. She didn't believe for one instant that Christine could be innocent. Perhaps,' Orloff added with a grim smile, '*she*'d have avenged herself on any man who jilted her. With the girl under arrest, she assumed any possible danger to herself was past. No, she went to meet someone connected with her precious deal. And that's a puzzle. What she was doing was illegal and possibly immoral, but I don't see a motive for murder in it.'

'Hélory? He might've wanted to grab the lot.'

'So he might, but I doubt if he'd run the risk. La Foucard had political clout, friends in high places. That's one of the reasons why we've never been able to nail her. Hélory knows she's protected. There'll be guys on my back tomorrow, if I don't find her murderer instantly.' Orloff sighed. 'To return to the matter in hand: for some reason, the murderer wished to dispose of the body.'

'Why go to all the trouble of hauling her up that cliff? If she was killed somewhere near the place where her car was parked, why not dump the corpse in the sea?'

'I think the idea behind dropping her into The Chasm was to confuse the issue for us, hopefully getting the death written

138

off as a suicide. The body sustained a lot of injuries after death.'

'That was some woman,' said Durieux with a graveyard grin. 'As a dead weight, she'd be a problem.'

'We're not looking for Superman. The evidence presented by the state of the clothes indicates that she was dragged, with the murderer clasping her ankles. The bruises show a sizeable hand, but not overlarge.'

'It's a steep climb.'

'On the popular path. What other ways up are there?' Orloff asked. 'There may be several. I want that place scoured for traces, including the route Christine used to reach the house.'

'*Merde*,' Durieux exploded. 'Don't tell me our operator had the nerve to drag his victim past the front door, while my dolts were in the kitchen, losing their shirts at poker. I'll see nothing's missed, Commissaire. We'll get on it right away.' He started for the door, then paused. 'The MO's exactly the same as in the murder of Luc Plouviez, only we haven't got the weapon. But if Marguerite Foucard was working on her deal, the crimes can't be connected.'

'Why not? Look at it the other way up. Suppose Luc's murder arose out of her deal?'

'But where's the motive in that? The stuff's still in Cyprus.'

'The link appears to be the house itself. Luc valued it to the extent of shutting it up for twenty years rather than sell it. La Foucard wanted it so that she could hide smuggled valuables. Who else was interested?'

'That guy we've got in the cells, and who we know for sure was at Devil's Bay that night, dossing down a stone's throw from where her car was parked: Pierre Basret.'

'It's time I had a word with him,' Orloff agreed.

'We've given him a shower, so he should smell a bit sweeter,' said Durieux with a laugh and went out.

Bernard de Montigny and Jacques Hélory encountered Anatole Plouviez on the steps of the hotel. He rushed up to clasp each of them by the hand.

'I was hoping to find you,' he gabbled. 'I can't tell you how distressed I am that Madame Foucard is dead. It's difficult to credit. She was so full of life. And then to throw it away! Why should she do such a terrible thing?'

The others exchanged glances.

'She didn't,' said Bernard.

Anatole's eyes popped. 'But I heard – '

'Forget it,' Hélory advised him. 'I've known Margot Foucard for more than twenty years. She was much too resourceful a person to contemplate suicide for so much as ten seconds. She was on top of the world. Everything was going fine for her.'

'I don't call having her fiancé murdered "going fine",' said Anatole in shocked tones.

'I'm talking about business, Monsieur. You may think that callous, but Margot had survived enough bad experiences in her life to take anything in her stride. She was angry at Luc's murder, but she wasn't about to break her heart over it.'

'It must have been an accident then,' Anatole said firmly.

'Margot wasn't the type to clamber over rocks in the dark,' Hélory replied with a grim smile. 'She was murdered.'

Anatole flinched. 'Are you sure?'

'Commissaire Orloff isn't committing himself, but he appears to be treating the case as a homicide,' Bernard told him.

Gloom settled over the man. 'When did it happen?'

'The night before last. Madame Foucard left here about eight – I saw her go – and she never came back.'

'She was supposed to meet me at nine, at the hotel,' said Hélory.

The information seemed to depress Anatole still further. 'Such a sad loss, she was a fine woman. This can only make matters worse,' he sighed. 'Monsieur de Montigny, I need your professional assistance.'

Hélory let out an unkind crack of laughter and seized the chance to escape. 'Don't forget you're representing me first,' he said, and made off across the square.

Anatole stared after him. 'Are you?'

'I don't think he'll need my services much,' Bernard replied. 'I doubt if there'll be a conflict of interests. If I find one, I shall be obliged to withdraw. What can I do for you, Monsieur?'

'It concerns my son. Perhaps you'd be good enough to come with me to my house. My car's here.'

Bernard's curiosity was aroused. There was quite a change in the man that morning. The self-important windbag was halfway deflated.

'Sacha is a disappointment to me,' Anatole said bleakly as they drove out of Tremerrec. 'I've built up a really good business here and he's at law school, but he's not shaping. He'll ruin everything I've worked for.'

It was the cry of many a parent. Bernard hoped that when his own infant son grew up, he would have the sense not to try living his life for him. He wondered idly what the Commissaire's father had said when the young Orloff elected to be a cop – and grinned inwardly at the fancy.

'He wanted to go to sea,' Anatole was saying. 'He just couldn't understand what a waste that would be. And then he took up with Christine Kergrist. I hoped he'd grow out of it, but he hasn't. He couldn't have picked anyone more unsuitable.'

'Wasn't it a relief that she preferred Luc?'

'That should have opened Sacha's eyes, but not a bit of it. He's besotted. This is the heart of the problem. Sacha hasn't got an alibi for the time of Luc's murder, and if Christine didn't kill him, it seems to leave only my poor lad as a suspect, the rejected lover. I tell you, Monsieur, 1 was shocked at the idea that the girl had done it, but that Sacha should be suspected – my God, he might even have done it! – it's killing my wife.'

Bernard uttered a sympathetic platitude and waited for the rest.

'It's her wish that you should represent Sacha,' Anatole went on. 'It's ridiculous, with lawyers in the family . . . My brother-in-law, Louis Tremel – you must know him – is first-class, and there are various cousins . . . but Yvonne insists on an outsider. Will you help us?'

'I'll do what I can, Monsieur,' Bernard replied, suddenly aware of being glad of an excuse to embroil himself further in the fascinating experience of watching Maximilien Orloff at work.

Pierre Basret was a sorry sight. The Commissaire felt a surge of irritation at the waste of a life. It was disgusting that a man of only thirty-two should have 'Old lag' stamped all over him. The future was an inevitable progression from one prison to another.

'What have you to say for yourself?' he barked.

'I've done nothing,' Pierre whined. 'Why pick on me?'

'You've been on the scene of two murders.'

'I never – '

'At best, you're a witness, Pierre. What about the night before last? What did you hear?'

'I was asleep. There's nothing else to do in that bloody hut.'

'You don't have to stay there.'

'And risk being picked up by you lot? I never laid a finger on Luc Plouviez. I didn't even know he was there. I thought the house was still shut up.'

Orloff pounced on the admission. 'Were you intending to have another look for the treasure?'

Pierre's mouth dropped open in blank astonishment, then bitter disappointment swept over him. 'They've bloody found it,' he exclaimed.

'Who are "they"?'

Pierre looked up in amazement that the question needed to be asked. 'That family. The bloody Plouviez. In the old days, Paul and Anatole were always hanging round in the hopes of finding it.'

'Are you suggesting that Anatole Plouviez has gone treasure-hunting again?'

'That old fart?' Pierre sneered. 'He wouldn't have the guts, without Paul to egg him on. It's Sacha you want. Shake the truth out of him – and the girl. They're in it together.'

'How d'you know that?' Orloff demanded.

'Stands to reason, don't it? They were there all the time, weren't they, sucking up to Luc, getting at him to wheedle out the secret of where the old man hid it.'

'Why do you think Luc would know?'

'He was the old man's heir, wasn't he? Why did he keep the place shut up all those years while he was away? He didn't want it, only what was in it.'

'If Luc Plouviez knew where this treasure was hidden, why didn't he have it taken out?'

Pierre's face took on a sly look. 'Didn't want to give anything to the bloody *fisc*, did he? He had to wait till he was fit enough to get at it himself. Ma says he had tools, she thought to rebuild the garden wall, but I wasn't fooled. I might've known I'd be too bloody late,' he added disconsolately and burst into tears.

Orloff sent him back to the cells to nurse his grief, called for his car to return to Devil's Bay. He felt a sense of urgency, of exhilaration even, which had little to do with the return of bright

142

weather after the rain of the previous day, and the warm sun shining out of a clear blue sky. The Commissaire was an old hand: he knew when a break was coming. Yet, behind the excitement, there was a certain sorrow . . .

Inspector Durieux squatted down to examine the latest find. 'The Commissaire will want to see this,' he announced. 'Call the office. And nobody, but nobody, sets foot on this spot.'

He stood up, gazing round. To one side lay the house; on the other, the fields of the Basret farm, with the pumphouse not many metres away. At his feet a rough path led from a secluded beach to the lane.

He could see it all now, as if he had been there when Marguerite Foucard was killed. All that was missing was the face of her murderer.

He watched his men at work, preserving the evidence, until the sound of a motor drew him away, back to the place where the dead woman's car had been found.

Orloff drove up, halting at the ribbon stretched across the lane. 'Progress? I received a message on my way here.'

The Inspector grinned. 'I've found the whole trail now, and you were right, it's not all that difficult. It begins here,' he said, as they drew level with the path to the house. 'This must have been the main entrance, once, with a gate in the perimeter wall. That's all fallen down now, and the gateposts with it. The gorse has taken over the remains. Our operator waited here.'

The Commissaire peered down at an area between two well-grown clumps of the spiky shrub, one embracing a rotting gatepost. The ground was beaten flat and scuffed.

'Not the most hospitable cover,' he remarked. 'But, after all, this is *la Côte d'Ajoncs*. So the rendezvous was virtually at the house, as I surmised.'

'The victim was attacked from behind and fell forwards, so she was making for the front door,' Durieux went on, pointing to marked places. 'Spots of blood along here, and a blob where the body was turned over for dragging away. There's a faint trail down this path.'

They trod carefully, keeping to one side, to reach the shore, where the men were examining the shingle.

'He used a boat,' said Orloff softly, leaping ahead of the evidence.

'That's right. It was pulled up on the beach – we've a few scrapes on the rocks – but there was no way of tying it up.' He snapped his fingers and was handed a small plastic envelope. 'The painter was secured under a boulder. Look at this: our old friend, the frayed rope.'

The Commissaire scrutinised the wisp of yellow fibre. 'You've done very well, Alain.'

'There's more. We've picked up the trail on the other side of the house. The boat was beached not far from where the sea enters The Chasm. It's not so steep a climb that way up, just longer.'

'Excellent. All we have to do now is nail our operators.'

The Inspector's eyes narrowed at the use of the plural. '*You know?*'

'I think so,' Orloff replied bleakly. 'I have to admit that I'm a little disappointed. But we still have some distance to go before I can make a move. I'm not taking any chances. I want to know the whereabouts of all members of the Plouviez family for the whole of yesterday evening, and also Hélory and Maître de Montigny. Check the boats too. One of them should have a frayed painter.'

Commissaire Orloff presented a forbidding face to Christine Kergrist. It wiped out her pleasure in seeing him.

'What's happened?' she exclaimed fearfully.

'Marguerite Foucard has been killed, battered about the head in exactly the same fashion as Luc Plouviez. You, Mademoiselle, are the only person I can place unquestionably at the scene of the first murder; equally, you are the one person who could not have committed the second. There is a symmetry in that which bothers me. However, that is not the reason for my visit. I have heard rumours of buried treasure at Luc's house. I discounted them, but now I've a witness who is totally convinced that this treasure exists. *Does it?*'

'Luc said so,' she replied readily. 'Uncle Emile told him.'

'Did Luc tell you where it is – or was?'

Christine shook her head. 'He didn't know. We were going to look for it when he was well enough. He thought it must be somewhere under the house, in the old foundations of the gun emplacement.'

'That house is full of valuable objects. Couldn't they constitute this treasure?'

'Luc wondered about that. He went through all those boxes of papers in the tower room to check. He could account for everything on the inventory the packers made when his mother closed the house. But there were still things missing.'

'Items which had been sold, perhaps?' Orloff suggested.

'No. Luc said Uncle Emile kept meticulous accounts, and every piece sold was marked off. These other things weren't.'

'Do you know what items are missing?'

'Jewellery and loose stones, old coins, gold and silver cups and plates, some pottery. Luc said it was very valuable stuff and should be in a bank vault. He made a list, you'll find it in the bottom drawer of Luc's desk.'

'That drawer is empty, Mademoiselle.'

'Then Luc must have put the list somewhere safe. In the tower, perhaps.'

The Commissaire's eyes held hers. 'Not in the tower, in the possession of his killer.'

Christine stared. 'Luc was killed for the *treasure*? That's mad. It mightn't be there any more.'

'You're contradicting yourself. You've just told me Luc believed it was still to be found, and you accepted his word. The matter has to be cleared up right away. You seem to be able to remember what was on that list Luc compiled, so you and I – and a few others – are going on a treasure hunt. We'll pick up your grandfather on the way. I'm told he knows all about the old gun emplacement.'

Henri Drouon pulled a wad of yellowed papers from his pocket, glanced round at the circle of interested faces, and laid them carefully on the table in front of him.

They had assembled in the entrance hall of Luc Plouviez's house: the Commissaire, Christine, Inspector Durieux and a couple of his men. All eyes were on the old man's hands as he spread his papers with loving care.

Durieux peered at them. 'What's all this?' The sheets were covered with pencil sketches. 'Diagrams? Of what?'

'It's a rough plan of the gun emplacement that was here during the war,' Drouon explained. 'It's not entirely accurate, the Germans weren't in the habit of handing out maps. This was compiled from notes surreptitiously made while it was being built.' From another pocket he produced an ordinary, large-scale map. 'Compare the two. You can work out where the underground tunnels run.'

Orloff pored over the maps. 'Didn't you tell me Basret *père* used one for storage? Which one?'

Drouon put his finger on the plan. 'That one. There was only a short stretch of it passable. Ten, fifteen metres at the most.'

'Where d'you reckon that would be in relation to this house?'

Drouon grinned. 'Right underneath.'

The Inspector was amazed. 'Don't tell me you extracted all this from Pierre Basret, *Patron*.'

'Hardly. But his obsession with buried treasure made me remember a little unaccountable detail,' Orloff replied. 'That was the traces of concrete on Luc Plouviez's slippers. Where had he picked them up? Not inside the house, yet he never went out of doors in them. Even if he had broken that rule, the soles would have had specks of sand, too, and there were none. Therefore he had been walking on dusty old concrete in a house where there was none.'

'He'd found the treasure,' Christine gasped.

'He'd found the hiding place, certainly – at a guess, that fifteen metres of tunnel. You'll find the tools he used in the kitchen, Inspector.'

Durieux went off at a run, returned with a crowbar and a chisel. 'I put these down to his working on the repair of the wall. What are we looking for? A trap-door?'

'I imagine so. It shouldn't be difficult to find. It has to be here on the ground floor. This is the part Emile Plouviez and his manservant built themselves.'

'He tiled the floor before the ceilings were plastered,' said Drouon. 'We thought it was because he didn't know how houses were built. Everyone was laughing at him. It never crossed our minds that the cunning old devil was concealing a trap-door. All we have to find is a section of tiles which haven't been grouted round the edges.'

'It'll be under a heavy piece of furniture,' Durieux prophesied. 'Where do we start?'

'Here,' said Orloff, laying his large hands on the table to push it against the far wall. He beckoned to the two detectives. 'You men move that chest.'

Slowly, the massive coffer was pulled away, and the dragons on the silk hangings seemed to writhe as a new draught caught them. The Commissaire examined the exposed floor.

'I think this is it,' he announced complacently. 'There are chipped tiles here, the marks of a crowbar, at a guess. We'll need the photographers and, probably, emergency lighting.'

The Inspector laughed. 'Do you have a crystal ball, *Patron*?' He went out to organise a team.

Progress was agonisingly slow, each step photographed and video-recorded. The trap-door was raised, revealing a black void, and the top rungs of a rickety ladder. A light was lowered. Dusty, decaying boxes came into view, some piled against the wall, others, lidless, scattered about the floor.

A fresh ladder was brought, and more lights, before Orloff and Durieux, accompanied by the photographers and the detectives, climbed down. Christine and Henri Drouon, unbidden, followed them. A policeman took a step towards the pair to send them back, but was stopped by a quick shake of the head from the Commissaire.

'This is old Basret's tunnel,' Henri whispered to his granddaughter. 'The entrance was over there.'

That end was blocked off by a roughly-made stone wall, the other stretched away into darkness. The air was still and cold. It felt like an ancient tomb.

'This is it, all right,' Durieux remarked, his voice echoing loudly, a violation of secrets. 'How did you drop on to it so quickly, *Patron*?'

Orloff shrugged. '*Par hazard*. I asked myself where I would site a trap-door. The entrance hall seemed the obvious place, with that chest to conceal it.'

Behind him someone muttered about people who could see through brick walls, followed by a quickly-suppressed snigger. Orloff ignored it, squatting down to examine the opened boxes.

'These appear to have been rifled. I wonder what was in them? These are the smallest boxes, presumably stacked on top of the others, and the first target of the thieves.' He called for a torch to scrutinise them. 'Ah, here we are. I couldn't believe that the careful Emile hadn't marked the boxes. This one bears a capital J. Mademoiselle Christine, recite me the small items on that list.'

Eagerly, she went forward. 'Jewellery, loose precious stones, coins.'

'That'll do for a start. Here's one marked "C". For coins. If these boxes were full, the thieves got away with a fortune out of these alone. Alain, have these gone over for dabs.'

The next box was marked 'P'. It, too, had been opened, but only half the contents removed. Gently, the Commissaire lifted out an object swathed in rotten sacking, which fell away at his touch, revealing a fat ginger-jar of a very pleasing blue with a delightful pattern of twigs bearing white blossoms.

'I think there should be two of those,' Christine said. 'Isn't it pretty? Is it very old?'

'Seventeenth century. K'ang Hsi period. As Luc said, a museum piece.'

She gazed at it. 'Wasn't that dish Luc used to keep on the table in the hall the same?'

'It was.' Orloff removed the lid, turned it upside down and laid it on the floor. It made a perfect little bowl. 'It's the cover of the twin to this one.'

'But that had been there for months,' she objected. 'Luc hadn't found his way down here before I went away.'

'It goes further back than that, Mademoiselle. The "bowl" was listed on the inventory raised at the time the contents of the house were put into store.'

Christine frowned. 'Why bring up just the lid? And where's the bottom part?'

'An interesting question. I'd like to know the answer to that,' said Orloff, signalling to the men to start unpacking the unopened boxes.

It was a slow process, each object being listed and photographed. Christine was set to writing down as much as she could recall of the missing list, while treasures were laid out on the dusty floor. The emergence of a solid gold dinner service sent Inspector Durieux off to arrange for safe-keeping in a bank vault.

Hours later, when the last box had been taken up and removed under guard, the tired and dirty team left the tunnel. The Commissaire let the men go, sent Henri Drouon home in a police car, but detained Christine and the Inspector.

'Sit down, Mademoiselle,' he invited, pointing to a chair against the wall opposite the still-gaping trap-door. 'I appreciate an opponent of intelligence and imagination, who presents me with a problem to exercise my wits. *As you have.*'

She had been staring in fascination at the black hole in the floor. Now, shocked, her gaze swung to his face, her mouth half-open to utter words which would not come.

'Believe me,' he continued. 'It's no pleasure to me to do this. I had hoped to work for your freedom, but justice has to be served.'

Beside Orloff, Inspector Durieux drew in his breath sharply.

Christine found her voice. 'I don't understand.'

'It was a clever plot, and daring, to use yourself as a decoy, the obvious suspect – you must have devised it, I doubt if Sacha's capable – and it nearly came off.'

She seized on one word: 'Sacha?'

'You had to have an accomplice, you could not do it alone – '

She jumped up. 'Stop! For heaven's sake, stop! Are *you* accusing me of killing Luc? I thought you were on *my* side.'

Chapter 12

Marcel Landais drew himself up to his full five feet five inches. 'My client is adamant, Commissaire. She maintains her innocence, in which I fully concur. I bid you goodnight. I shall be back in the morning,' he added and stalked out.

'He's changed his tune a bit,' Durieux growled. 'That's the one who was advising her to plead guilty. Damned if I know what to think myself.'

'I can put together a reasonable case against Christine and Sacha working as a team,' said Orloff, as if talking to himself. 'The motive is the treasure, once Luc had found it – which we know he did. Sacha is the person he'd be most likely to tell, the only member of the family he liked.'

'La Foucard was hoping to stash her stuff in that tunnel,' the Inspector reminded him.

'I doubt if she knew what was already down there. Luc was a close-mouthed fellow. It was Sacha and Christine who needed money, so that he could be independent of his father and they could marry.'

'Local opinion has the girl genuinely in love with Luc.'

'The gossips aren't always right. It might have been an elaborate game to gain his confidence. That's the line I'm obliged to take.'

'Why don't we pull the boy in now, *Patron*?'

'Because I'm not ready,' the Commissaire replied shortly. 'Sacha does the job, while Christine is pedalling across the landscape in as noticeable a costume as one could wish for, bound to be seen. Sacha hears her knock at the front door, the signal for him to leave through the kitchen. She hangs about in the house for a while, making sure Luc is dead, handles the poker to draw suspicion on herself, and would have raised the alarm if La Foucard hadn't walked in on her first. Are you with me?'

150

'Yes,' said Durieux, gloomily.

'Then Anatole Plouviez puts a spanner in the works; he sends Sacha off to Rennes before he has had time to carry out the second part of the plan – the killing of Marguerite Foucard which is bound to be linked to that of Luc and will put Christine in the clear. But the crime *is* committed, you note, as soon as Sacha has an excuse to return to Tremerrec.'

'And then we have another spanner in the works when Pierre Basret blows the gaff about Uncle Emile's treasure and Sacha and Christine suddenly have the sort of motive judges and juries like: money,' said the Inspector, sighing heavily.

'To hear you, anyone would imagine you'd like them to have got away with it,' Orloff snapped.

'Sacha doesn't have an alibi for last night, either,' Durieux continued grimly. 'Not until late, when you caught him dogging your footsteps. All we have to do is find where he's stashed the loot and we're home and dry.'

With a crashing oath, the Commissaire jumped to his feet. 'I'm a dolt. What about the fingerprints from the tunnel, Alain?'

'They aren't fully processed yet. So far, there's been nothing but unidentified ones and a few of Luc's.'

'What about the empty boxes?'

Durieux reached for the telephone. 'I'll check. They're working late.' He spoke into the receiver, listened, then announced, 'Nothing for us there. All unidentified. What the hell? Sacha would wear gloves.'

Orloff shook his head. 'That's not the point. The dust on those boxes was as thick as everywhere else, *inside* as well as out. That's what was bothering me. They weren't emptied in the past few weeks. More like many years ago, at a guess, immediately after Emile Plouviez and his manservant were drowned.'

Durieux sat up. 'That's only twenty years back. Whoever did the job might still be alive. How many more people know about that damned treasure? There was plenty left in the tunnel to go back for.'

'And never a chance to get at it,' Orloff agreed. 'The house was boarded up and swathed in barbed wire, until Luc came back.'

'Where does that leave Sacha and Christine?'

'That remains to be seen,' said Orloff with a grim smile. 'It'll keep overnight. Tomorrow should be an interesting day.'

For Maximilien Orloff it began at five o'clock, when he was summoned from his bed and whisked off in a police car to Devil's Bay. The causeway was littered with cars and vans.

Alain Durieux materialised out of the grey dawn. 'The lad on watch got bored and decided to start the search of the rest of the tunnel, which was the day shift's job. He's found something.'

The tunnel was full of light, and as he climbed down the ladder cameras flashed at the far end, where the passage dipped deeper into the earth, ending in a wall of fallen debris. A group of men stood there, parting to let him through. Orloff found himself face to face with the eminent professor of forensic medicine who had done the post-mortem examination on Marguerite Foucard. Beyond him, at the foot of the wall, lay two skeletons, neatly laid out side by side. Rags of clothing hung on the bones, and the remains of serviceable men's shoes enclosed the bones of the feet.

'Two males, fully grown, elderly,' said the pathologist. 'Different racial types, one Caucasian, the other Asian. I think there are fractures to both skulls. I'll be able to see better when I get them upstairs.'

'Henri Drouon says there are German soldiers down here,' said Durieux in the Commissaire's ear.

'Not these,' Orloff replied. 'Look at the boots. Those aren't German army issue.' He squatted down beside the remains for a moment, then gave orders for them to be removed, when the photographer had finished.

There was a small tinkling sound as the larger skeleton was transferred on to a sheet. Work halted immediately. Orloff pushed rags of clothing gently aside, revealing a key lying on the vertebrae. Tweezers were placed in his outstretched hand.

'At a guess, that came out of a waistcoat pocket,' he murmured, holding it up. He glanced at Durieux. 'What room here doesn't have a key?'

'The one up the tower, *Patron*. It was lost.'

'And now found. Try it, Alain.'

Durieux raced off. In the quiet of the underground tunnel, he could be heard pounding up the stairs. Then came a great shout.

'I thought so,' said the Commissaire. 'What we have here are the remains of Emile Plouviez and his manservant, Lim.'

'They were lost at sea,' one of the detectives, a local man, exclaimed.

'Ha!' said the pathologist, who was already examining a skull. 'This one didn't drown. He died of multiple fractures of the skull. Let me have a look at the other. Yes, him, too. You should look for a weapon.'

It was found in minutes, lying between the wall and the second skeleton: a crowbar, one end encrusted with dried matter beneath the dust.

'I don't think it's been wiped,' the pathologist remarked, inspecting it. 'We should get blood samples from that. And fingerprints. Treat it gently.'

Orloff nodded. 'Identification procedures have to be followed, but I've no doubt in my own mind as to whom we have here. What interests me now is why they're here and not at the bottom of the sea. Come on, Alain, let's see if Henri Drouon is up and about. He must know the details of the shipwreck they were supposed to have died in.'

The old man was in his kitchen. They accepted a cup of coffee and the Commissaire explained what they wanted.

'That was a long time ago. A sad business for the Plouviez family,' Drouon said. 'What does it matter now?'

Orloff told him.

The old man brightened. 'Murdered, you say?'

'Without a doubt. I'm sure you understand my interest in how the story got about that they were lost at sea. Do you think you could reconstruct the events for me? For instance, can you pinpoint the day Emile and his man died? Take your time.'

'It was January,' Drouon said, after a while. 'Paul's body came ashore on the 25th. I remember, because of it being the feast day, the Conversion of St Paul. My father's name was Paul, so we used to have a special dinner for his feast – ah, but you don't want to hear about that, only the way it fixes the date. I missed most of the celebrations.'

'How long had he been in the water?'

'He'd been gone a couple of days, and his mother was sick with worry. With hindsight, it's easy to see how we were all deceived. Paul was doing odd jobs for Emile Plouviez. He was missing, so was Emile. The house was locked up and there was no sign of the

153

servant. And the boat had gone. Putting that together meant all three had gone sailing.'

'What about the wreckage of the boat?'

'That was found on the 24th, when the search parties set out. By the time the alarm was raised on the 23rd – the last day any of them was seen – it was too dark to do anything. The boat had a great hole in its side, and no survivors had been picked up. Everyone knew they were lost.'

'What sort of weather was it?'

'Blowing up to a storm, on the 23rd. We thought they'd been fools to put out in a small boat with a high sea running.'

'Didn't anyone wonder why?'

Drouon shrugged. 'Folks had ceased to wonder at anything Emile Plouviez did. He was an original.'

'I had the impression that he only went sailing with Luc. Paul had a different character. He has been described to me as a layabout.'

'He was an idle bugger,' Drouon agreed. 'After Luc had gone to sea, his mother pushed Paul into making himself useful to Uncle Emile. I reckon she knew about the will, that Luc was due to inherit the lot, and she wanted her precious Paul to have a share. It looks as though he decided to help himself.'

The Commissaire ignored the invitation to speculate. 'So the murders of Emile Plouviez and Lim took place no later than January 23rd. Have you any idea when they were last seen? I realise it's asking a lot, after twenty years.'

'Ah, but I do know,' said the old man triumphantly. 'The morning of the 23rd, I had to go halfway to Tremerrec to take down a poor fellow who'd hanged himself. His wife had died, and he couldn't bear it. I'd been at school with him, too. It was a bad day, that. The point is, Commissaire, I met Emile Plouviez and Lim on the road home – on their bikes, as usual, but Lim had picked up a puncture, and they hadn't got a repair kit with them. It was a Saturday, they were dressed up in their best clothes for their weekly trip to town. I offered to take them to the village to get the tube patched, but Emile said it wasn't worth the trouble, he'd changed his mind about going to Tremerrec, and he'd rather have a lift home.'

'You're a marvel, Monsieur,' said Orloff, as Drouon paused for breath. 'I wish all witnesses were as clear-minded.'

154

Drouon beamed. 'All part of the service, Commissaire. I reckon I was the last person to see them alive. Apart from Paul, that is. He'd been working at the house that morning, and he'd know they meant to be away for most of the day. But they came back early, thanks to that puncture, and found him pillaging the underground hiding-place.'

'You've got it all worked out,' said Durieux in some admiration. 'Paul killed the pair of them and then rigged up a scenario to make it look as though they'd been lost at sea.'

'Except that the last bit went wrong,' Orloff pointed out. 'Paul can't have intended to kill himself, too. Where was the boat washed up, Monsieur?'

'At Pointe du Château,' Drouon replied promptly, 'a few kilometres up the coast. Emile's cap and Lim's scarf were found at separate places between here and the Pointe.'

'And Paul's body?'

'On the other side of the Château, in the estuary,' Drouon replied, turning bright eyes on the Commissaire. 'Do I have to keep quiet about all this?'

'For the moment, yes,' Orloff told him with some regret, then, on second thoughts, relented. 'But only the deductions about the involvement of Paul Plouviez. I don't wish that to become common property just yet. But you may talk about the discovery of the treasure, that is sure to jog memories.'

They left behind them a happy old man, impatient for his neighbours to get up out of their beds.

'There're no flies on Henri Drouon,' the Inspector remarked. 'He was on to the truth like a shot.'

'There are a couple of loose ends,' Orloff replied.

Durieux cast his mind over what the old man had said. To his annoyance, he failed to pinpoint the omissions. 'Such as what?'

'The loot, for one. Only small, high-value portable and readily saleable items were taken, but judging by the size of the boxes, it was no small amount. Where is it?'

'After twenty years, who knows?'

'There's no record of it ever being found. Unfortunately the list of the contents of those boxes is missing, but it's just possible we can reconstruct it.'

'How?'

'By going through the receipts in the tower room. Old Emile

never threw a thing away. There's a chance that some or all of the transactions relating to that missing stuff might be up there still.'

'Wouldn't Paul have thought of that and destroyed them?'

'There's no evidence that he knew what was in that room. On the contrary, the key was in the pocket of the man just murdered. Paul didn't even look for it.'

'Agreed, but what's the point, Commissaire?'

'Suppose that, over the years, those valuable little items had – very gradually, so as not to provoke comment – appeared in collectors' hands.'

Durieux stared, then snorted, 'I'm an imbecile. There was an accomplice. It follows, *hein*? How does one man kill two others without help?'

'The existence of an accomplice is a reasonable inference; someone to make off with the loot while Paul fixed the "wreck". One wonders, who?'

'Pierre Basret? He'd be twelve at least, probably strong. And he's obsessed with that treasure. If he were the accomplice, he'd know there's a lot more down in the tunnel.' He shot a glance at the Commissaire's face. 'What else have you up your sleeve, *Patron*?'

'The curious fact that Paul Plouviez was drowned.'

'What's wrong with that? He was fixing a cover-up of his crime and got caught in his own trap.'

Orloff shook his head. 'I don't buy that. The Plouviez are a bright lot. All we know about Paul is that he was idle. There's no suggestion that he was a halfwit. That family may despise their fisherfolk ancestry, but they love the sea and all of them sail. Even in desperate conditions, Paul would have known it was too dangerous to put out to sea.'

'What else could he do?'

'When we talk of things being washed up, we mean they are found on the beach,' said Orloff obliquely. 'It's assumed that the sea has deposited them there. Tell me, is it possible to walk along the beach from here to Pointe du Château?'

'I used to do it regularly when I was a boy, hunting for things in the rockpools. It's not easy walking when the tide's in, you have to clamber over the rocks, but it is possible.'

'Even dragging a small boat?'

'Good God,' Durieux exclaimed. 'That's the way to stage a shipwreck in a storm, without getting your feet wet. No one would doubt that a smashed boat and the personal effects of its passengers had been washed up. Then Paul would only have to go a short way out into the sea to soak his clothes to back up his story. I suppose he thought the estuary side of the Pointe was the safest place. More fool him, there are bad currents there. What do we do now? Take Basret apart?'

'All in good time,' said Orloff calmly. 'We've prepared only part of the case. Tell me, what is a reasonable deduction to make from a series of murders in a given location, all of which have been carried out by the same sort of weapon, in this instance an iron bar?'

Durieux's eyes widened. 'The same operative, of course. You take my breath away, Commissaire. Are you suggesting it was Paul's accomplice who bashed in the heads of Uncle Emile and his man – and *is doing it again*?'

'Bear with me while I fly up into the stratosphere, Alain. Up till now there has been no satisfactory motive advanced to account for Luc Plouviez's murder, other than a vengeful jilted lover – Sacha or Christine – or both out to steal. Charities don't go in for polishing off benefactors, and I don't fancy anyone doing him in for a forty-second share of the contents of the house. Above ground, that is. Below ground is a very different matter.'

The Inspector was listening intently. 'The easily disposable stuff had been taken out. Shifting the rest on the quiet would require an organisation.'

'You're thinking of our shifty antique dealer?' said Orloff with raised brows. 'A case might be made, but I'm not talking about another robbery. There's something much more important: two dead men. Luc knew the treasure existed. More, we know he'd found the entrance to the tunnel. He went down there the day he died. And that's why he was killed. He had a list of what was supposed to be in the tunnel – which the murderer removed – so he would discover the robbery and, sooner or later, he was bound to come across the murder victims, too.'

'That house was shut up for twenty years. Why didn't Paul's accomplice get in there and remove the evidence?' said Durieux. 'Oh, wait a minute. Basret did have a go, and after that the place was festooned with barbed wire so that not even a cat could get in. The balloon would go up once the charity got the place, surely?'

Orloff smiled. 'What would they do with that house? It's too small to use as a convalescent home.'

'They'd sell it. La Foucard was after it.'

'So she was. She knew about the tunnel. Luc had promised to store her "family heirlooms". But she was second in the queue. Anatole Plouviez, the executor of Luc's estate, was there before her. And he had been Paul's best friend,' the Commissaire added, softly.

'The accomplice,' growled Durieux. 'Then that phone call Luc made the Saturday before he died was to tell Anatole he'd found the tunnel, and would open it up for Marguerite Foucard's inspection when she arrived on August 15th.'

'Now you're with me, Alain.'

'How do we prove any of this, *Patron*, short of catching him with some of the stolen goods, and they'll have been sold long ago?'

'We can have a try. Where do you fit in the little blue and white bowl, the cover of the K'ang Hsi ginger-jar?'

The Inspector jumped. 'I was forgetting that. I found it in her handbag, where she'd stashed it when we came over here to pack the clothes she'd left upstairs. Remember how she shot ahead of us, leaving Bernard de Montigny to act as porter, and was standing in the hall, waiting with a martyred look on her face? Why did she want it?'

'As an instrument of blackmail. Because she knew where the bottom part was.'

'How could she? She was a virtual stranger round here.'

'The only place we know she has visited, apart from the hotel and this house, is the offices of Anatole Plouviez, where her lawyer had the use of temporary accommodation. I infer that the rest of the jar is there. With her interest in and knowledge of *objets d'art*, she'd recognise it at once.' The Commissaire sighed, then said, 'She wouldn't know what she was doing, of course. All she was interested in was her smuggling venture. She was putting the screws on to make sure she could buy the house, and she went to a rendezvous in all innocence, probably lured by a false promise of showing her the tunnel. She would have no idea she was meeting a murderer. Poor, dashing Marguerite. What an end!'

'Shall I pull Anatole Plouviez in?' Durieux asked eagerly.

'We'll do it together. At this stage, we have very little evidence. First, get hold of Maître de Montigny, show him the bowl and ask

158

him where the body of the jar is. He's an observant fellow, he'll know. Next, set up surveillance of the Plouviez house and office. Very discreet. How is that boat check getting on? I must have that one with the frayed painter found. And put someone to dig in the archives to find the report on the death of Paul Plouviez and on the wrecked boat. Then clean yourself up and meet me at Anatole Plouviez's house at nine o'clock.'

Bernard de Montigny was not at all pleased to receive a telephone call in the middle of his breakfast, least of all from his young client's father. Bernard had suffered from a feeling of impending doom ever since a brief but sinister interview with Inspector Durieux shortly after seven o'clock, concerning, of all things, a Chinese ginger-jar. It was bizarre in the extreme, but the fact that his late client, Marguerite Foucard, had bothered to steal the lid of the object made him uneasy. A picture swam into his mind of her clutching a fat-bellied vase. And then he had been sworn to silence . . .

'What can I do for you, Monsieur Plouviez?' he enquired as politely as he could manage.

Anatole's agitated voice came over the wire. 'Commissaire Orloff is coming here at nine. I'm very much afraid he intends to arrest Sacha. Please come, we need you.'

With a sigh, Bernard promised, knowing he would be failing in his duty if he did not. He rather liked young Sacha, and had sympathy for the boy. Life could not be easy with Anatole Plouviez for a father . . . He ordered a taxi for eight thirty.

Four people were waiting for him: Sacha and his father, and two women.

'My wife,' said Anatole, and the smaller of the ladies stepped forward to offer her hand.

'Monsieur, please do what you can,' she pleaded, tears drowning anxious hazel eyes. Yvonne Plouviez was too thin, and her shoulders drooped, perhaps from the burden of being Anatole's wife. She had no colour in her face, and her fair hair hung lank, yet she must have been pretty in a chocolate-box style in her youth.

'And my sister, Madame Tremel,' Anatole swept on, as the other woman all but elbowed her sister-in-law out of the way. Yvonne sank modestly into eclipse.

Bernard's hand was crushed in a grip as strong as any man's as an Amazon bore down on him. Recoiling slightly, he professed himself enchanted. Fascinated would have been more accurate, for Simone Tremel was a larger edition of her brother, but with an altogether stronger face. This was the one who should have been the man of the family.

Introductions were barely over before the doorbell rang, and the Commissaire, accompanied by Inspector Durieux, was shown in. Orloff never had difficulty in dominating a room, and that day he seemed more forceful than ever.

'I bring you some news,' he announced when all were seated. 'A discovery was made yesterday at Luc Plouviez's house. There is a trap-door in the entrance hall which gives access to a section of one of the tunnels bored during construction of the gun emplacement which stood there during the war. In the tunnel was found a number of boxes containing objects of high value, which have now been placed in safe custody in a bank vault.'

'The treasure!' Sacha exclaimed, and was silenced by a black look from his father.

'Precisely,' said Orloff and handed a typed sheet to Anatole. 'As executor of the estate, here is a list of the items which will be released when the investigation is concluded.'

Four pairs of eyes glued themselves to the paper, as Anatole read it. 'I don't know what to say, Commissaire,' he said, looking up. 'I'm utterly amazed.'

His sister snatched the list, Yvonne and Sacha leaning over her shoulders to take a look.

'How do we know it's all here?' Simone demanded belligerently.

Anatole, petrified at the implied slur on police honour, started to protest, but Orloff cut him short. 'Everything was unpacked and checked in front of witnesses, not only police, but bank officials, Madame,' he said coldly. 'However, there is evidence that part of the hoard had been stolen. Some boxes had been emptied, others opened and part of the contents removed. I should tell you that Luc Plouviez had in his possession a list of the entire collection. The missing items are readily portable: mainly jewellery, loose stones and ancient coins.'

'You should have sent for one of us,' Simone declared. 'I shall lodge a complaint.'

'I am conducting a murder investigation, Madame – a broader one than I anticipated. I have to inform you that the tunnel also contained the remains of two dead men. I expect to be able to identify them as Emile Plouviez and his manservant, Lim.'

Yvonne screamed, and Sacha put his arm round her. Anatole gaped, dumbstruck.

'They were drowned,' Simone snapped.

'No, Madame. Each one was struck on the head with a crowbar. Murdered.'

'But Paul went out in the boat with them. What about him?'

'What, indeed, Madame? Since, apparently, he rigged up a "shipwreck" to conceal the actual manner of death of his uncle and the servant, the inference is that Paul was the murderer.'

The green tinge on Anatole's face ebbed away as Simone gave forth: 'I never had a great opinion of Paul, but I'm shocked that he would commit such a crime. I suppose there will be some unpleasant publicity over this. We shall have to put up with it.'

'The position is a little more complicated,' Orloff replied silkily. 'This crime casts a long shadow. I am satisfied that both Luc Plouviez and Marguerite Foucard were murdered because of their knowledge of the tunnel and its contents.'

His words produced an uproar which died down as suddenly as it had arisen, leaving only Simone Tremel declaring, 'It's not possible. Paul's dead.'

'But his accomplice isn't,' said Orloff. 'Luc's list was removed, and, I imagine, destroyed by his murderer. Fortunately, we have a witness who has been able to tell us some of the items on it, and, at this moment, a complete list is being prepared from receipted bills of sale found in Emile Plouviez's archive in the tower room. Two items have been identified already. One of them is in this room.'

He paused to let the information sink in. No one uttered a sound or moved. The Commissaire left his chair and strode over to the master of the house.

'Monsieur, how do you account for having in your possession a gold stater of Philip of Macedon?'

Anatole gaped at him. '*What?*'

In one swift movement, Orloff snatched the heavy gold ring off his finger. 'Perhaps you never realised what it was. Or how rare. This is from the fourth century BC. I see it has been properly mounted, so that both sides are visible: on the outside, the reverse of the coin, showing a two-horse chariot with prancing steeds, and inside, the obverse bearing the portrait head of the king. One such coin is missing from Emile Plouviez's collection in the tunnel, and I am taking you into custody for questioning in connection with the murders of Emile Plouviez, his servant Lim, Luc Plouviez and Marguerite Foucard. Under the powers vested in me as an official of the *police judiciaire*, this house will be searched and also your offices. The keys, if you please, Monsieur.'

Dazed, like a man in the grip of a nightmare suddenly come true, Anatole handed them over.

Yvonne fainted.

Chapter 13

It turned out to be a long session. Shortly after midnight, Anatole Plouviez took refuge in tears and lamentations, and Orloff called a halt to the proceedings. He left the interrogation room to break the news to Bernard de Montigny, dragooned against his instincts but persuaded by the agonised pleas of Yvonne Plouviez, to watch her husband's interests.

'We can all go to bed now, Maître.'

Bernard jumped up. 'He's confessed?'

The Commissaire shook his head. 'No. Can't you hear him?'

'What have you done to him?'

'He hasn't been beaten with rubber hoses, if that's what you're implying. Your client has had enough and is staging that exhibition to oblige me to make an end. We're all tired. I shall resume in the morning.'

'It's already that,' said Bernard sourly. 'What time?'

'Nine o'clock. You may see Monsieur Plouviez now, if you wish.'

'I suppose I'd better. Will you give me a lift back to Tremerrec? I drove over in Plouviez's car and you've impounded that.'

'It will be my pleasure,' the Commissaire replied. 'But we won't talk shop. You may bring me the latest news of our mutual acquaintances.'

He was rewarded with a suspicious glance and went off, smiling, to have a final word with Inspector Durieux, who, in turn, was not overpleased with the great man when he learnt that he was to meet Orloff at seven thirty at the place where Paul Plouviez's body had been found. He took a small revenge by giving the Commissaire the dusty report on the death of Paul Plouviez, just unearthed from twenty-year-old files, knowing that Orloff would read it before he slept.

* * *

In the early morning the beach was deserted. There was an expanse of sand, and rocks where wading birds hunted for food, with the inevitable gorse growing right to the shoreline. The river, narrowing beyond the bridge at Tremerrec, here was a broad estuary, the land on the other side half hidden in mist. Behind the beach rose the headland and the trees surrounding the nineteenth-century château, now a hotel.

Orloff paced about. He estimated that, crossing the neck of land, the place where the boat was found could not be more than a kilometre, perhaps less. Looking upriver, as far as the eye could see, were houses scattered along the shore, each with its own landing-stage. Yachts rode at anchor.

Inspector Durieux arrived, his car bumping along a rough track through the gorse. Spotting the Commissaire, he halted and jumped out, walked down to the beach, stopped and turned at the sound of another engine behind him. It was a third police car.

'Now we're all here,' said Orloff, as the driver emerged.

'Kergrist?' muttered Durieux. 'What's he doing here?'

'There's no better-qualified man to tell us about the habits of this river. He must have fished out many bodies over his years in Tremerrec.' He advanced to shake hands with the Brigadier. The Inspector hurried after him.

Orloff was explaining what he wanted. 'Tell me, Brigadier, if a body was washed up here, where's the most likely spot for it to have entered the water?'

'Anywhere upstream,' Kergrist replied promptly. 'There's a strong current.'

'Oh, my word,' Durieux groaned. 'Don't tell me they made a cock-up of that report.'

Kergrist frowned. 'What's that?'

'I'm obliged to take a close look at the death of Paul Plouviez,' Orloff said. 'His body was found here. He was supposed to have drowned when a small boat foundered during a storm at sea.'

'My God, I remember that, though I wasn't on the case. There were two other victims, one of them the guy that lived at Devil's Bay, Luc's uncle.'

'Those two weren't drowned,' Orloff told him. 'Their skeletons were found yesterday in an old tunnel under the house. You may well look astonished, but this might be good news for Christine.'

164

Kergrist could not disguise an explosion of hope and joy. 'Really? I'll do anything. Just tell me what.'

'Right now I must sort out this drowning, which may seem irrelevant but is not. With the accident somewhere out at sea, would you expect to find a body here?'

'Possibly. The sea does strange things. With the currents as they are, it'd have to be a freak, but storms break the rules.'

'Thank you. Now, can we try to set limits to the area from which the body could have entered the water?'

The Brigadier frowned, puzzled. 'Falling off a boat, for example?'

'No. I was thinking more along the lines of falling off a landing-stage,' said Orloff blandly.

Behind him, Durieux choked on bitten-back words. He coughed to cover the sound.

Kergrist shot an inquisitive glance at the Commissaire, waited for an explanation which did not come, then said, 'It wouldn't be far downstream. See that island? Just upstream of that there's a small peninsula. Anyone falling beyond that would be caught by it.'

'How far away is that?'

'Three kilometres.'

'Are there houses built on it?'

'Only one,' Kergrist replied. 'It's a small estate called La Roche Blanche. There's a landing-stage and a boathouse but no boats. Two very old ladies live there, sisters, both widows.'

'There'll be other places between here and the peninsula,' Durieux chipped in. 'But after twenty years no one's going to remember if Paul Plouviez was seen thereabouts.'

'Those old ladies will,' said Orloff. 'They may be old, but they're not senile, and they are members of the Plouviez family.'

'Would you like me to knock them up?' Kergrist offered eagerly.

The Commissaire shook his head. 'They'll keep until later. It's time to wrap this case up. I've everything I need now. I invite you to join us, Brigadier. I'm sure Inspector Durieux will not object to your being in at the kill.'

There was a line-up waiting for them: Yvonne Plouviez, and Sacha, accompanied by Bernard de Montigny. Courteously the Commissaire had them brought into his temporary office.

Bernard acted as spokesman. 'We have some evidence to lay before you, concerning the whereabouts of Monsieur Anatole Plouviez on the morning of August 15th.'

'Are you presenting me with an alibi, Monsieur?'

'Yes, he is,' Sacha broke in and, ignoring his mother's hand pulling on his sleeve, rushed on, 'He really was trying to find me, Commissaire. He does, you know. Every time we have a quarrel and I split, he searches the town. He fusses about me like an old hen.'

Yvonne winced at the phrase and tugged harder at her son's sleeve, insisting in a stage whisper that he leave the talking to the lawyer.

Sacha shook himself free. 'Let me tell it my own way, Mama. Papa's afraid I'll end up on the drug scene. He thinks, just because the guys I hang out with wear their hair long and make tears in their jeans they must be addicts or pushers or both. He'll have to eat his words now. He owes them. Four of them were in the bar on the wharf that morning. They saw him arrive – you can't miss his Mercedes, it's the biggest model, there's nothing like it in Tremerrec. Papa was there until at least twenty-five past ten, when he went to the Cathedral.'

'Is that it, this alibi?'

'Isn't it enough?' Sacha demanded hotly.

'It hardly improves your own position, young man. You haven't an alibi at all, unless you can find some conveniently-placed friends to stand up as witnesses for you. Will your hippy friends testify?'

'Yes, they will. I'm not going to let my father be accused of a murder I know he didn't do. There's bound to be someone who saw him in the Cathedral, too.'

Orloff glanced at Yvonne. 'Is that your cue, Madame, to produce a handful of witnesses?'

She flushed. 'Not at the moment, but I agree with Sacha, some will be found if we try hard enough. My husband's very well known.'

'The Cathedral was crowded that day?'

'Packed,' she replied. 'We arrived at the last minute; the upset between Sacha and his father flung us all into confusion. It threatened to become a general row, with the aunts bringing out

166

old grievances and Louis Tremel making it very clear that even after twenty years, he still thinks he married beneath him – '

'Bravo, Mama,' Sacha cried. 'Wash all our dirty linen in public.'

'Be quiet,' Orloff commanded. 'I understand your mother's anxiety. Please continue, Madame. I need to know everything that happened in the minutest detail. Now, your husband had taken the Mercedes, Sacha was away in his car, how did all of you travel to the Cathedral – not surely all in one car?'

'We took mine, too,' she replied, impatiently. 'Louis drove it, I was too upset. Parking was a nightmare, and we had the aunts to cope with, and then we couldn't find seats all together. I was so distracted, I couldn't pay attention to the Mass, dreading the trip down the river and the barbecue. I knew it was going to be a disaster – and it was – then, to crown all, the woman sitting next to me collapsed and caused a terrible commotion. And at the same time, poor Luc was being killed, too. But not by my husband. Or my son,' she ended defiantly.

'I still require witnesses, Madame. When the unfortunate lady was taken ill, didn't you look round for your husband, for help? I'm sure you weren't just standing by while your neighbour was in distress.'

'Of course, I wasn't. I held her until the first-aid man could get through the crowd. Yes, I did look for Anatole, but by that time the aisle was jammed.' She hesitated, then said sadly: 'Commissaire, I'm sure you're a good judge of men. You must have realised that my husband talks big – '

'Yeah, a windbag,' Sacha muttered.

Orloff's gaze flickered over him. 'Don't try to pull the wool over my eyes, young man. You and your father fight, but he was trying to protect you, and now you're returning the compliment. Please continue, Madame.'

'What I'm trying to tell you is that Anatole likes to think he's a great man. He cuts a dash and makes out he's a Casanova, but it's all winks and nods, and I don't think he's ever done more than pinch an occasional bottom.' She broke off, as tears flowed.

'This is painful for you, Madame,' said Orloff gently.

Yvonne mopped her eyes. 'Not as painful as having Anatole accused of murder. I'm trying to explain to you that he couldn't have killed Luc or Marguerite or anyone. It's not in him. He'd yell at them or play dirty tricks to get even if he thought they'd done him down. He wouldn't have the courage to pick up a poker and hit anyone. I know my husband, Commissaire. I know his faults and his virtues. He rescued his father from debts and disgrace, he scraped up the money for his sister's dowry, he's been a good provider and he loves his children, and I love him. Simone will be here soon, and she'll tell you. Anatole's weak and all that bluster is to cover it up.'

There was a short silence while Yvonne wept into her handkerchief. Sacha stared at the floor.

Then Orloff addressed Bernard. 'I accept the evidence about the bar, Monsieur, subject to obtaining statements from the young people concerned. We shall have great difficulty in tracing everyone who was in the Cathedral.'

'With your permission, I'll advertise,' said Bernard.

'It may not be necessary,' the Commissaire said, earning a sharp and interested glance from the lawyer. 'While Sacha is here, I have some questions to put to him about his boat.'

The young man looked up. 'What about it?'

'Traces of blood have been found in it, of the same group as that of Madame Foucard, also a thread from her dress.' Sacha stared at him openmouthed, not believing what he heard. Orloff went on, 'She was struck down at the landward entrance of Luc Plouviez's house, then dragged to the nearest part of the beach. Traces of that journey are in your boat. The painter is badly frayed and fragments of it have been found on the shore at that place, and also on the other side of the house, in Devil's Bay, where the boat appears to have been beached so that the body of Madame Foucard could be unloaded and thrown into The Chasm. Shreds from the painter were found during the examination of the scene of Luc Plouviez's murder, clinging to the mooring-ring at the back of the house – '

He got no further. With a great cry, Yvonne launched herself at her son, to fold him in a tight embrace, screaming defiance at all the world.

Inspector Durieux rushed in, followed by two of his men.

'Get them out of here,' Orloff commanded. 'I'll speak to them again when Madame has calmed down.'

'What's going on?' demanded a loud and authoritative voice, as

Simone Tremel strode in, brushing aside divers police officers who were attempting to prevent her from storming the Commissaire's sanctum.

Orloff roared above the din. 'Everybody out. That includes you, Madame, unless you wish to see the inside of a cell.'

It was Simone's turn to stare. In all her life no one had ever dared to speak to her in such a way. Alain Durieux seized the opportunity to bundle her out of the room.

If anything, Anatole Plouviez looked worse than the night before. No sleep had relieved his torment. He gazed at Orloff out of lacklustre eyes.

'This is the moment of truth, Monsieur,' said the Commissaire mercilessly. 'Our laboratory technicians have worked through the night. Now I am sure that I have the whole sequence of events. Let me explain the position to you.'

He paused, but Anatole offered no response, hardly hearing him. At his side in the interrogation room, Bernard de Montigny sat alert and watchful.

Orloff continued, 'Four murders have been committed. Two, years ago, the others recently. They are intimately connected, all perpetrated by the same person. Twenty years back Emile Plouviez and his manservant returned unexpectedly to their home and discovered thieves in the underground store room. They were struck down, their bodies left in the tunnel, while a bogus shipwreck was staged to cover their disappearance. No one had any suspicions until Emile's heir, Luc, came to live in the house. Luc knew the underground hoard existed and, being a trained Intelligence officer, eventually discovered the entrance to it. More, he wished to help the woman who had saved his life when he was blown up. She needed a place to keep valuables: what was more natural to offer her room in the tunnel, particularly since he felt in honour bound to offer her marriage in accordance with a somewhat foolish promise he had made to her. The situation was complicated by the fact that Luc had fallen in love with a lovely young girl.'

Anatole looked up. 'Christine killed him. Of course, she killed him,' he said, as if repeating something learnt by heart.

'No, Monsieur,' said Orloff sharply. 'Kindly pay attention. Luc was killed because he was proposing to open up the tunnel. The next victim was Marguerite Foucard. This lady's plans had been ruined by Luc's murder. She still needed a hiding-place for her treasures and time was pressing. Luc had a list of his uncle's hoard in the tunnel. Marguerite had seen this, so when she spotted a piece of that collection, above ground, and in a place where it should not have been, she saw an opportunity for a little blackmail.'

Anatole still gave no sign that he was listening, but he stiffened in horror when the Commissaire produced a bag and from it drew out a ginger-jar, complete with lid.

'Yes, Monsieur, you recognise this, don't you? Madame Foucard had seen the body of this in your office waiting room, and Luc had used the lid to hold loose coins. She knew there was a pair of these jars on Emile's list, and no sign of the other jar in the house. Therefore, she reasoned you had obtained it from the hiding-place. It followed that you knew the way into it, but had not told Luc. La Foucard knew how to put two and two together. She understood that you had guilty knowledge and she proposed to cash in on it. What she didn't know was that this jar had been obtained at the price of the lives of two men. What had you used it for? The transport of coins and loose precious stones? Your mistake was leaving the lid upstairs in the entrance hall, where it was listed on the subsequent inventory as a "Chinese bowl".'

Anatole shook his head, but in an unconvincing manner.

'The blackmail attempt backfired on her, as might be expected with a bold murderer, maddened that after all these years, danger of exposure should suddenly threaten. Marguerite was lured to her death. That murder led to the disclosure of her business activities and indirectly to the discovery of the tunnel and its contents. Also, it pointed directly to you, with the ginger-jar and the gold coin mounted in your ring, flaunting your crime. I recognised that coin for what it is the first time I saw it, and wondered how it came into your possession since I saw no other signs of an interest in or knowledge of antiquities.'

'I bought it,' Anatole gasped.

Orloff laughed. 'That's not an item you'd find in a junkshop. Can you produce a bill of sale? No, I thought not. But it's the jar that nails you. It sets you at the scene of the murders of Emile Plouviez and Lim. You and your cousin Paul.'

Anatole was sweating freely. He goggled at Orloff.

'Yes, Paul Plouviez. It's time we thought about him. If you didn't murder those men, then he did. But Paul is dead, and a dead man couldn't take your son's boat and tie it up at the back of Luc's house and murder him, slipping away out of the back door while Christine was knocking at the front. Nor could he use the boat to ferry Marguerite Foucard's body round to the foot of The Chasm. Yes, Monsieur, you have something to say to me?'

'Sacha's boat?' Anatole demanded hoarsely. 'It's impossible.'

'On the contrary, I can prove it.'

Anatole's face was chalky and great globules of sweat stood out on his brow. Orloff judged it the moment to pounce.

'Let me tell you something else, Monsieur. I misled you when I said there are four murders. There are five. And the fifth victim is Paul Plouviez, your once-best friend.'

Anatole started to his feet. 'No, that's not true. He was drowned.'

'Certainly, but not by accident out at sea. That boat trip never happened. The "wreck" was staged. I've been reading the report on Paul's death. There were unexplained marks on his body, put down to other persons in that ill-fated boat clutching at him in their desperation. Those bruises were made when his murderer attacked him from behind and held him under the water until he was dead. At the landing-stage at La Roche Blanche.'

Anatole shook his head. 'Oh, no, it wasn't like that. You can't pin that on me. Paul had to risk putting out to sea, in spite of the weather. We were supposed to meet at La Roche Blanche. He never turned up.'

'Because he was dead before you arrived. Dead and on his way downstream to fetch up on the beach under the Pointe.'

Anatole gasped. 'But why? No, I can't believe it. Why should Paul have to die?'

Orloff jerked his head at Inspector Durieux, who slipped out of the room. 'You may ask that question of the one person who knows the answer, Monsieur,' he said, as Durieux brought in Yvonne, Simone and Sacha. 'Now.'

For a moment, Anatole stared at his family, then the words began to gush out. 'I've covered up long enough for you.' He pointed a shaking finger at his sister. 'This is all your fault. I wasn't the one who struck down Uncle Emile as he climbed down the ladder, nor Lim when he came to look for him. I didn't want the old man's treasure. You're the one who was so desperate to buy yourself a husband. But you've gone too far. Why did you have to use *my boy's boat*? And why did Paul have to die? Wasn't he the one who'd given us the chance to get at the treasure? Why, Simone, why?'

His sister rounded on him. 'Shut your damned fool mouth, you'll ruin the lot of us.'

'It's too late,' he panted. 'The Commissaire knows.'

'I suppose you've told him,' Simone spat back. 'Paul would never have kept his trap shut and he'd have tossed his share around like there was no tomorrow. He was no loss, and no one would have believed he could have swum ashore in that sea.'

'He was my friend.'

'And a right pair you've turned out to be. I should have dealt with you, too.'

'I don't understand,' Anatole gasped. 'You told me Paul would go out in the boat.'

'I was protecting you, booby, from your own sentimentality. The wreck had to be faked to make sure the "remains" were washed ashore. And that included Paul. You always were a fool, Anatole.' Simone whirled round to confront Orloff. 'And how did you know?'

'I had been told that you and your brother and Paul did everything together, Madame,' he replied coolly. 'Also that you were the dominant one. I suspected there might have been more than two robbers. It needed a quick and resourceful mind to devise an immediate plan to cover the murders. You were the obvious choice. But it was the use of the boat which fixed it on you. Sacha was always obliged to lend it to you every year when you came on holiday to stay at La Roche Blanche. He was sent off to Rennes immediately after Luc's murder, and did not return until this week. The boat was forgotten. It was recovered from La Roche Blanche yesterday evening. It was most ingenious of you, Madame, to capitalise on the confusion in your brother's house on the morning of August 15th. You knew Luc had found the tunnel and was intending to open it. He'd told your brother. Isn't that so, Monsieur?'

'When he phoned on the Saturday,' he agreed dully. 'I passed the news on to her. I didn't know what we were to do.'

172

'She did. I'm told the Cathedral is always full to overflowing on that feast-day. Your sister came every year, so she knew she could drop her passengers at the door, then go away on the pretext of finding somewhere to park. But what she did was drive straight back to La Roche Blanche, take the boat, kill Luc, and was back in Tremerrec in time to mingle with the crowd coming out of Mass.'

'Prove that!' she flung at him.

'Never doubt that I will. Tell me about that Mass, Madame. Where were you sitting?'

'I stood at the back. Near the door.'

'Did you see anyone you knew?'

'I haven't lived in Tremerrec for nearly twenty years. I've lost touch. I can't say I saw any acquaintances.'

'Not even your own brother? He was at the back, too.'

Simone dismissed it. 'The place was packed. There were a lot of people standing at the back.'

'And do you recall anything special happening?'

She scented a trap. 'Not particularly,' she said, between her teeth.

'Not even a woman collapsing? Do you know which way she was carried out?'

She shrugged. 'I take no notice of interruptions.'

Orloff turned to Anatole. 'Monsieur, did you inform your sister of Marguerite Foucard's blackmail threat?'

'I asked her what we should do. She said she'd think about it.'

Simone screamed, 'Shut up, idiot. Don't imagine they're going to let you go free by trying to blame me.'

'I'm not depending on accusations,' said Orloff, smiling. 'We have found an iron poker this morning in the boiler room of La Roche Blanche. It has yielded bloodstains and fingerprints. As has the crowbar from the tunnel underneath the house at Devil's Bay. Inspector, the *juge d'instruction* is waiting for these beauties. Escort them to him, will you? I'll follow shortly.'

'Yes, Commissaire, at once,' said Durieux jauntily.

Simone Tremel, ready to battle to the last, marched out ahead of him.

Anatole hung back. 'I would like to make a statement, Commissaire.' He glanced painfully at his wife and son. 'I

173

should like my family to hear what I have to say, if that is permissible.'

Orloff nodded, waving them to chairs at the side of the room, and switched on the recording-machine. 'Maître de Montigny, too?' he enquired, with a sidelong glance at Bernard.

'I hope he will consent to represent me,' Anatole said quickly, 'when he has heard what I have to say.'

Bernard sighed. 'Oh, very well. I suppose you want me to put in a plea of mitigation.'

'There are grounds, I assure you,' Anatole replied. 'My position is this, Commissaire: I admit I went with my sister and my cousin Paul to plunder Uncle Emile Plouviez's hoard. This was over twenty years ago. He had refused us, all three, financial help. Simone needed to bring a fat dowry to the Tremels; Paul wanted to set himself up in business; and I was saddled with my father's debts. I'd paid off what I could, but it had left us so poor I couldn't even afford to run a car – I cycled to the office, pretending the exercise was good for my health – and my mother was in distress. I'm not offering this as an excuse, just as a fact. Paul had discovered the way into the tunnel, and we chose a day when Uncle Emile and Lim would be away. They came back unexpectedly and caught us.'

He paused, lost in the horror of remembrance and needed a prompt from Orloff to resume the sorry tale.

'Simone picked up a crowbar and hit Uncle Emile with it. He fell off the ladder and she hit him again, several times.' Anatole passed his hand over his face. 'I was stunned. I stood there, not believing my eyes. Then we heard Lim come out of the kitchen and exclaim at the trap-door in the hall being open. He came down and the same thing happened to him. I was in a panic. Simone poured the old coins into one of the Chinese jars – the box was too bulky to take – and told me to go to the office and hide it there, while she and Paul cleared up in the tunnel.'

'Why did you leave the lid behind?'

'It wouldn't fit into the saddlebag of my bike, so I left it on the hall table. Simone took the jewellery – I don't know what Paul had – and I gave her the coins the next day. I didn't want any of the valuables, not with blood on them.'

'You kept the jar.'

'I thought it was worthless.'

'And one coin.'

'I found it under my desk days later. It must have rolled down when we emptied the jar. I didn't know that it was of any great value, either.' Anatole swallowed rising sobs. 'I thought it would make some amends if I took nothing, even though I needed money. I couldn't inform on my own sister. And there wasn't anything to be done for Uncle Emile and Lim.'

'There's such a thing as decent burial,' Orloff remarked.

'Simone said Paul had taken the bodies out to sea to stage a shipwreck. I never doubted it, or that Paul had himself perished in the storm.'

'When did you find out where the bodies were?'

'Very recently, Commissaire. Simone was furious when she found out that Luc had left the house to a charity. She badgered me about buying it – I had my own eye on it, to make it into holiday flats – and then she told me what was in the tunnel. Even then, it never occurred to me that she'd killed Luc – or Marguerite Foucard.'

'She could not have afforded either of them to go down the tunnel, could she?' said Orloff tartly. 'Do you expect me to believe you hadn't figured that out, Monsieur?'

'It's the truth,' Anatole insisted. He shot an anguished glance at his wife and son. 'I'm sorry, Yvonne. Sacha, look after your mother.'

The Commissaire turned off the recorder and rose to leave Bernard alone with his clients.

Sacha made a dive to head him off at the door. 'What about Christine?'

'She's free. I doubt if she will hold anything against you personally.'

'She'll never love me,' the young man cried desolately.

'Probably not. But she'll still be a good friend. Settle for that,' Orloff advised him and went out.

Several people were waiting for him, but his eye was taken by a small group of three: two men, one tall, one short, and a radiant girl, who ran forward to meet him.

'What's happened?' Christine demanded. 'I thought I was lost – and Sacha, too – then, suddenly, everything is changed and I am free.'

Her father and her lawyer followed on her heels. Marcel Landais bustled forward importantly.

'All charges against my client are being dropped, Commissaire?'

Orloff looked down on the little man, mildly amused by this belligerence. 'Yes, Monsieur. She leaves with no shadow of stain upon her character.'

Landais beamed and took Christine's hand in a distinctly possessive manner. She disengaged herself gently, with a ravishing smile.

She had not finished with Orloff. 'You really thought I'd lied to you, didn't you?' she challenged him.

'Momentarily. I was delighted to prove myself wrong, Mademoiselle,' he replied with a glimmer of a smile.

'What about Sacha?'

'He's in the clear. Does that satisfy you?'

She would have asked more, but her father, inarticulate for once, was offering broken thanks to the Commissaire. Orloff waved them away.

'We can all get on with our lives again, my friend. Please convey my salutations to Madame Kergrist.'

Christine tugged at his sleeve. 'Come home with us. Just for an hour. Don't run away from us yet.'

He shook his head. 'I've been here longer than I intended. I must return to Paris, where a rather nasty corpse is waiting for my attention. As for you, young lady, go back to your studies. I might need a good doctor in my old age,' he said, and turned away.

He came face to face with Bernard de Montigny.

'That was a bravura performance, Commissaire. My felicitations.'

'All in a day's work,' Orloff replied with a glint in his eye. 'So is the paperwork. There will be a mountain of it. I must make a start. Give my regards to your mother when you see her.'

He strode off down the corridor, well aware that he had left Bernard grinding his teeth. The thought – and all that lay behind it – amused him.